Mara Geist

ADELE GRIFFIN

Witch Twins

W9-CPB-490

Illustrations by Jacqueline Rogers

HYPERION PAPERBACKS
FOR CHILDREN
NEW YORK

For Tessa and Tanya

Text © 2001 by Adele Griffin
Illustrations © 2001 by Jacqueline Rogers
All rights reserved. No part of this book may be reproduced or transmitted in any form or by any means, electronic or mechanical, including photocopying, recording, or by any information storage and retrieval system, without written permission from the publisher.
For information address Hyperion Books for Children, 114 Fifth Avenue, New York, New York 10011-5690.

If you purchased this book without a cover, you should be aware that this book is stolen property. It was reported as "unsold and destroyed" to the publisher, and neither the author nor the publisher has received any payment for this "stripped book."

First Hyperion Paperback edition, 2002
3 5 7 9 10 8 6 4 2
Printed in the United States of America

Library of Congress Cataloging-in-Publication Data
Griffin, Adele.
Witch twins / Adele Griffin.
p. cm.
Summary: Troubled about being separated at school and preoccupied with sabatoging their father's marriage, ten-year-old witches Claire and Luna have little time to think of something good, smart, and tricky to do that will finally make them one-star witches.
ISBN 0-7868-0739-3 (tr)— ISBN 0-7868-1563-9 (pbk.)
[1. Witches—Fiction. 2. Twins—Fiction. 3. Remarriage—Fiction. 4. Weddings—Fiction. 5. Family Life—Pennsylvania—Fiction. 6. Schools—Fiction. 7. Pennsylvania—Fiction.] 1. Title.
PZ7.G881325Wi 2001
[Fic]—dc21
00-63385

Visit www.hyperionchildrensbooks.com

ALSO BY ADELE GRIFFIN

Witch Twins at Camp Bliss

☾

Amandine

Dive

The Other Shepards

Sons of Liberty

Split Just Right

Rainy Season

Contents

1

Butterflies and Bad News

LUNA AND CLAIRE BUNDKIN were identical twins. Their hair was the color of maple syrup and their eyes were the color of warm chocolate chips. The only way to tell them apart was by the tiny chicken pox scar just beneath Luna's chin, but not many people knew about that.

They both loved-loved-loved gymnastics; their teacher, Mrs. Sanchez; and all flavors of

Schmidt's ice cream (except vanilla bean, which was just okay). They both hated-hated-hated swimming parties, indoor recess, and avocados—although Claire hated avocados more than Luna did. She said she could start gagging at the very smell of them, although Luna insisted that avocados don't really have a smell. Claire answered that if she got even a smidgen of slimy avocado taste on her salad it would make her throw up. But Claire could be very dramatic like that.

And, oh yes, they were witches. But more about that later.

They were both age ten (Luna was thirteen minutes older) and had lived in Philadelphia, at 22 Locust Street, for their entire lives. Over the years, their narrow sandstone townhouse had been through some changes. Some changes were big; other changes were small.

For example, four years ago, lightning had split the Bundkins' only real-live locust tree, which used to stand handsome as a doorman in its cutout sidewalk rectangle at the bottom of their front steps. Their mother had cried almost a whole day about that, because the tree was more than one hundred years old and a monument. Now it was just a stump, slightly improved when Justin, their big brother, had carved BUNDKIN RULES! into the top of it with his fishing knife. (Well, he always said he didn't do it, but it was such a Justin thing to do that everybody is still very suspicious.)

Then, three years ago, their parents had got divorced and their father had moved out of 22 Locust Street and bought a small house out in Rosewood, which was half an hour away in the suburbs. Their mother had cried longer than a day about that, and their father had cried, too, and so had Luna, Claire, and Justin, because the Bundkins had been married for fifteen years and besides, divorce is tough, go ask anyone.

But then, two years ago, their mother had met her boyfriend, Steve, who was a chef at The Aubergine, one of the fanciest restaurants in town, though Steve was more a jeans-and-sneakers kind of guy. And last year, their father had met his girlfriend, Fluffy.

Yes, she really was called Fluffy. But more about her later.

The most recent change to 22 Locust Street had been this past November, when their mother had bought new living room curtains. They went from blue stripes to red and green flowers. It was a small change, but it really spruced up the room.

This year, so far, nothing much had happened at 22 Locust Street. In fact, most of winter had been pretty boring. No surprises. No disasters, or surprising disasters. Not even a single snow day, Luna mentioned.

"Which is too bad," she said. "Snow days are sooo romantic."

"We still could have one. It's only the middle of March," Claire said. "Remember, March goes out like a lion!" She growled and made claws.

"No, March comes *in* like a lion and goes *out* like a lamb," Luna corrected.

"Well, it feels like it came in like a turtle,

and it's staying a turtle," Claire responded.

Luna looked up at the gray March sky. She and her sister were standing outside on their front steps waiting for their father, who was taking them (plus Justin) to his house in Rosewood for the weekend. If it didn't rain, they would get to go horseback riding at Puddinhead Farms.

Only right now it looked like rain.

Claire looked up, too. "I should run inside and get my umbrella," she said.

"You mean *my* umbrella," Luna corrected. "You lost yours two weeks ago on the field trip to the Art Museum, remember?"

"I did not," said Claire, but she didn't put any stomp in her words because Claire was always losing one thing or another.

"Did too, and you know it!"

"Did not, and you married it!"

Luna put her hands on her hips.

Claire put her hands on her hips.

"Stop copying me," said Luna.

"Stop copying me," mimicked Claire.

Luna frowned and turned away. Claire could be the world's worst tease, and sometimes the best thing to do was to ignore her. She touched her finger to her chicken pox scar, which she'd had for almost half of her life. ("You shouldn't have scratched," their mother always said. Jill Bundkin was a doctor and knew a lot about things you shouldn't scratch.) Luna liked to feel her scar, though, because it reminded her that she looked a teeny bit different from her sister.

On the outside, it was (almost) impossible to tell Claire from Luna.

On the inside, however, Claire and Luna were as different as the sun and moon, peaches and peanut butter, or long division and poetry. For example, right now, while Claire probably was thinking up other ways to tease her sister, Luna let her mind wander to imagining her favorite thing, her wedding.

Luna liked to imagine her wedding a lot. Obviously not the groom part, because she thought most boys were grubby and she would never choose to spend a lifetime with one, even a mature one with sideburns and a cleft chin. It was the other parts of the wedding she liked best, the spun-sugar cake and the rose-and-baby's-breath bouquets and the bridesmaids in their bell-shaped, swoopy dresses, with the softest, swoopiest dress of all reserved for the bride, along with a handmade lace veil so beautiful it could break your heart.

No wonder everyone cried at weddings.

Luna squeezed her eyes shut to concentrate on the most important part of her wedding—the dress—and she got such a perfect picture of its swoopiness that butterflies fluttered in her stomach.

Blleeeep! The sound of a car horn startled her from her thoughts. She opened her eyes to see her father's car pull up to the curb.

"Hey, gals!" Fluffy grinned and waved from the passenger seat. A big diamond ring flashed on her finger.

Luna's wedding butterflies went from a warm flutter to a cold flop.

She knew what that ring meant.

"Waiting long? Where's your brother? Does anyone have the correct time? Are you bringing just these two bags?" Their father, Louis Bundkin, was a newspaper reporter for the *Philadelphia Inquirer*, and he liked to ask lots of questions all at once.

Fluffy waved again from the passenger seat. Neither twin waved back, because they did not especially like Fluffy. She was nice enough, but she was also big and loud and liked to wear bright clothes and she usually called them "sugar" or "gals."

But Fluffy did not seem to notice any unfriendliness.

"We thought we'd take you all to Licks 'n' Sticks for dinner!" she said as the girls climbed in. "It's a celebration!"

"Licks 'n' Sticks!" yelled Justin from the roof, where he was playing hacky sack. "I'll be down in a jiff!"

"Can I get two Hawaiian sticks and no vegetable sticks?" asked Claire.

"Can I get three Chinese potsticker sticks and no vegetable sticks?" asked Justin, who had made it to the car in less than a jiff.

Luna said nothing, even though Licks 'n' Sticks was her favorite restaurant. She nudged her sister and pointed to Fluffy and mouthed the word *ring*, but now Claire was too busy elbowing Justin for space to pay Luna any attention.

Why am I always the one to notice disasters? Luna fretted as she snapped on her seat belt. Fluffy's ring was the worst thing to happen this year, and so far she was the only one to see it.

At the restaurant, Luna could not concentrate on enjoying her dinner. Not her skewered pineapple-, green pepper-, and lamb-on-a-stick, not her broiled potatoes-on-a-stick, not even her hot fudge sundae (which was not served on a stick, because Schmidt's ice cream desserts were the "Lick" part of the menu).

Every time her eye caught sight of Fluffy's flashing diamond, Luna felt completely sick.

"Fluffy and I have an announcement to make," their father said after their sundaes were scraped to the bottom and he had ordered his usual after-dinner coffee. He reached across the table and took Fluffy's hand. "Fluffy and I are getting married."

"I knew it," mumbled Luna.

"Congratulations! Can I have a dollar for the video games?" asked Justin.

"Congratulations," said Claire. *Fluffy, blech!* said her eyes to Luna across the table. But it was only a small *blech*, because Claire did not know what trouble they were in for.

"Justin, we'd like you to be your dad's best man, and I hope both of you gals would be my junior bridesmaids," said Fluffy. "And of course, I'd looove your advice on everything—the dresses and food and flowers. Oh, a wedding takes so much darn planning!"

"We might be busy," said Luna.

"I'll be glad to work around your schedule, sugar," said Fluffy, not noticing Luna's rudeness. "'Course, I'd been thinking about doing the whole shebang out in Texas. But that seemed kinda complicated."

"Do whatever you want, Fluff," said their father. "Just tell me where and when, and I'll show up."

His words froze Luna to her seat. She could hardly speak for the rest of the evening.

It was not until late that night, after all the good television was over and Fluffy had driven back to her home in Chestnut Condominiums and everyone else had gone to bed and all the lights were off and Justin had stopped bumping around in the next room playing hacky sack, that Luna spoke her fears out loud. She was very wide-awake, anyway, because it was hard to fall asleep without the soothing city noises of police sirens and garbage trucks around her.

"You know the worst thing about Fluff, don't you, Clairsie?" she whispered across to the other bed.

"No, what?" Claire whispered back.

"She's from Houston, Texas."

"Oh, blech!" exclaimed Claire. Then she asked, "What's wrong with Houston, Texas?"

"What's wrong with Houston, Texas? It's two thousand miles away, that's what! Crumbs, Clairsie, you can be thick! Don't you get it? You heard Dad. 'Just tell me where and when, Fluff, and I'll show up!' He's under her spell! He'll do whatever she wants!"

"Like the zombietrons on *Galaxy Murk*," gulped Claire. (*Galaxy Murk* was the only television show that Justin and the twins agreed on. It came on Thursday nights at eight.)

"Except that this is real life." Now Luna began to say out loud every single thing that she had been worrying over all night. "The way I see it is, after Dad and Fluff get married, she'll probably want to have a baby. And when it's born, she'll give him some Texas name, like *Houston*. Then, when he's big enough, Fluffy'll want Houston to rope dogies and wear spurs and a cowboy hat like all the other Texan boys and girls. Little by little, she'll convince Dad that the only way Houston'll be truly happy is if he's living in the *real* Houston, with her family and friends and all. And—poof!—see, Clairsie? Dad is as good as gone."

"Gizzards and grapes, Fluff is as good as stealing our dad," said Claire, forgetting to whisper and sitting upright in her bed. "I might have to boycott her." Claire had just learned the word *boycott*, and in Luna's opinion she was sort of overusing it. So far tonight, Claire had boycotted a broccoli-on-a-stick and all of Justin's TV-show choices.

"Shhh." Now Luna sat up in bed, too. "Claire, keep your voice down, or Dad will hear."

"This is so unfair!" Claire punched her pillow. "You know, I never did like that sneaky old Fluff. She thinks she's a real princess just because she works at a fashion magazine. But I was looking through her purse tonight, and she has lots of dis-*gus*-ting habits. For one thing, there's so much hair clogging up her brush you wouldn't believe it, and I also found a bunch of candy wrappers, and a tissue with some smeary lipstick in it, and a gummy yucky Life Saver way down at the bottom of—"

"Claire, you really shouldn't sneak through other people's things," said Luna sternly.

"Loon, what are we going to do? She's gonna run off with our own dad!"

Luna was silent, thinking.

Outside, a low wind had kicked up, and the patter of a cold, dark March rain began to *plink* and then to drum on the roof. It was not until Luna spoke in her grave, almost-one-star-witch voice that she knew she was making the decision that had been brewing inside her all night.

"Methinks we will have to call on Head Witch Arianna."

And just saying the words out loud gave Luna a little shudder. It went right from the top of her head all the way down to her toes.

Calling on Head Witch Arianna meant that this was serious business.

2
Three Times Uncharmed

HEAD WITCH ARIANNA was also known as Grandy. She was Claire and Luna's grandmother, and she lived way out in the country, in Bramblewine, Pennsylvania. To get to Bramblewine, Claire and Luna had to take the Septa local train from Philadelphia's Thirtieth Street Station, heading west. The train stopped twelve times before Bramblewine. By the thirteenth stop, the twins were always the last two passengers on the train. (In fact, most people did not even know there was a thirteenth stop.)

Claire liked how Bramblewine station was weedy and run-down. Spooky! It would have been kind of cool and kind of scary to be stuck here all alone. Luckily, Grandy was always waiting for them in her long, black Lincoln Continental, a car so old that Claire and Luna's mother remembered riding around in it when she was a girl.

"And that is another strange thing about your grandmother," Jill Bundkin mused. "I've never known anything of hers to break down. Not that rambling old car, not the toaster; why, there's never even been a leak in the roof, and that sure is one crumbly house that I grew up in. Things ought to be running to ruin."

What their mother did not know (and Claire and Luna did) was that Grandy was a five-star witch. So as soon as any of her things started to get old or worn-out, Grandy simply repaired them with spells. Repair spells are the simplest kind, so easy even a baby witch could do them. For example, how hard is it to clap your hands three times and say:

I call upon the Kitchen Fixer.

Recharge yourself, electric mixer!

But their mother did not have any idea about repair spells, because she herself was not a witch. (Most everyone knows that witchcraft, if it runs in a family at all—which is rare—most often skips a generation. It is a very recessive gene.)

For as long as they could remember, on the first weekend of every month, the twins had visited Grandy out in Bramblewine. Grandy herself rarely came into the city, not for any witch-based reason, but because she hated pigeons. "Their awful red eyes and feet! Their garbage-eating ways! Give me the grace and beauty of a hummingbird any day!" Grandy always said.

Justin used to come along, too, but last year he had joined the debate team, and now he was busy with weekend debate competitions. Well, that was his official excuse, the one that the twins were instructed to give to Grandy, but really there wasn't much for Justin to do out in Bramblewine. No neighbors, no television, not even a basketball hoop for entertainment.

"Bramblewine is bo-ring," Justin said, "and I can't play hacky sack for a whole entire weekend."

But if you're a witch, Bramblewine is one of the most exciting places in the world. It is like traveling to the Great Barrier Reef if you are a scuba diver, or to Colorado if all you love to do is ski and hike. Not only does it have ideal stargazing skies, but it is also a habitat for more witch-friendly species of mushrooms and flowering plants than anywhere else except, reportedly, a remote island off the coast of New Zealand.

"Off to Bramblewine," said Claire happily as the twins sat together on the train the weekend after what they both referred to as Bad News Night. "Grandy will know what to do about old Fluff." She squeezed her sister's hand reassuringly. Luna could be a worry-wart.

"I just hope it's okay to go during a *middle* weekend," worried Luna. "As long as I can remember, we've gone on the *first* weekend of the month."

"Grandy said it was fine," said Claire. "You're such a worrywart."

"Am not."

"Are too."

"Am not, I was crossing my fingers against what you said."

"No crossies count, no takebacks," said Claire quickly.

Luna stuck out her tongue and Claire stuck out hers.

Luna rolled her eyes and so Claire rolled hers back. She knew it annoyed Luna when she copycatted.

"Maaaaay-rose!" called the conductor, stepping into the car as the train heaved to a stop in front of the flagstone station that marked

Mayrose. Claire stared out the window and counted as a dozen people got out. Five minutes later, the conductor shouted, "Silvertoad!" and six more people stepped off the train.

Now there were two stops left before Bramblewine; Langham and Dillweed. Claire counted as three more people detrained in Langham. That left the usual last person, an elderly man wearing a felt hat and a pea coat on the train bound for Bramblewine. He was sound asleep as always.

And just as the train creaked around a narrow bend, the man woke up with a start. Just as he always did.

"Diiiiill-weed!" hollered the conductor as the train rolled to a stop. Claire watched as the man touched his hat, collected his newspaper, and departed.

Poor man. He always looked sad to get off the train, Claire thought. Sad, and a little confused.

And now (as always) she and Luna were left all alone.

After Dillweed, the countryside changed. The trees became taller and twistier, the grass grew wild and curled like seaweed. Birds seemed to know things; their eyes watched roundly down from high, bare branches. Even the train itself seemed to feel the extra effort to get to Bramblewine. Its wheels ground heavily on its tracks; it squeaked and hissed a final weighty sigh as it pulled into Bramblewine station, which was just an unmarked tin shed and a wooden bench.

As was his habit, the conductor did not even step into their car for this last stop. His voice floated vaguely from somewhere up front.

"Braaamble-wiiine . . ."

"I see Grandy!" Luna picked up her overnight bag and jumped down the aisle and out the door. Claire knew that her sister was a scaredy-cat as well as a worrywart and was always nervous to be alone on the train. Claire, who wasn't frightened at all, followed casually behind.

Grandy was waiting in her Lincoln Continental. Her Maine coon cat, Wilbur, was curled up in the back seat. Grandy herself was dressed up in a tasteful dark suit and silver star earrings. She looked businesslike and slightly preoccupied as she gave each twin a birdlike peck on the cheek.

"Be extra sweet to Wilbur. Yesterday, he ate a quarter pound of dryer lint, thinking that it was a mouse, and he hasn't been himself since," she told them.

Wilbur opened one glossy green eye, yawned, and then settled back into sleep. He was sixty-eight human years old and could eat anything, and he was almost never awake. Secretly, Claire hoped that when the time came to get her one-star-witch kitten, it would be a whole lot cuter than fat, bored Wilbur.

"Grayer than gray makes a beautiful day," sang Claire as they sped along one of the hundred long, snaking country roads that led to Grandy's house. In Bramblewine, none of the roads was marked, but all of them could lead you to where you needed to go if you concentrated hard enough.

"Claire, please put on your seat belt," ordered Grandy.

"You're not angry?" asked Luna. "That we came in the middle of the month?"

"Of course not," snapped Grandy. "It's always scrumptious to have my twinnies with me."

Claire crossed her eyes and stuck out her tongue at Luna as if to say *I told you so*, although she was not convinced. She could tell by Grandy's distracted face and slightly grumpy mood that this weekend just might be the wrong time to ask Grandy for a favor. Especially a witch favor.

With witches, timing is everything.

The car pulled up the rutted drive that wound all the way to Grandy's house. The driveway was filled with several other musty, dusty, dark old Lincoln Continentals.

"What's going on?" asked Luna.

"Didn't I tell you? I'm hosting a retreat,"

said Grandy. "Just a gathering of some of my nearest and dearest of the coven. Tonight's topic is about saving the Goodacre Nature Preserve, where we hold our annual Inspirational Tales Evensong. And to think those greedy developers are trying to replace it with a car dealership! Well, they don't know what they're up against." She got out of the car and slammed the door so hard it creaked and fell off with a thunk.

Quickly Grandy snapped her fingers and cast:

Oh, what a bore—

Repair yourself, door!

And the door jumped back to place and rebolted itself to its hinges, good as new.

Grandy was a whiz when it came to spells.

She'll fix the Fluffy problem, easy, thought Claire.

In the kitchen, Claire's nose (which was good enough to smell an avocado) picked out crescent cookies, sugared popovers, and chicken soup made with garlic, rosemary, barley, and allspice. She could also sniff out that all of the food had been made with spells. It had that special, no-mistakes whiff to it. Regular cooking was filled with spill smells and burn smells and oops-I-added-an-extra-teaspoon-of-lemon-zest smells.

Witch creations, on the other hand, were perfect right down to the last minute and milligram.

Voices flowed from the parlor. Loud, bossy voices. Grandy's nearest and dearest had been around for a long time, and they all had a lot of opinions.

"Don't be shy, you know the gang." Grandy shooed them. "I'm just going to doctor up this dinner. We'll be eating in a few minutes."

"Grandy, will we have some time alone with you, later?" asked Luna. "Because we have a terrible prob—"

"Anything you have to say can wait until later," said Grandy. She sniffed first with one nostril, then the other. "Go, twins, go."

Which was actually a little spell, as Grandy had sniffed them right into the parlor. The other witches were upon them instantly.

"Well, if it isn't our favorite twin set!"

"My, how they've grown!"

"Come closer, let's see your palms!"

And so Claire and Luna were passed and poked and prodded as Grandy's friends Diana, Aerianrhod, Isis, Demeter, and Mikki all grabbed at their palms and looked into their eyes, trying to tell their fate and fortune.

"You'll have to let me cast your runes," exclaimed Isis. She was a magnificent old witch who, it was rumored, had stopped the last two hurricanes that had swept the Carolinas. "I've got some sublime new stones."

"And I'll read your cards," said Diana, who was Grandy's oldest friend from college and the most elegant of all. Diana had long, gray hair that she kept in a twist, and she was always wearing something snakeskin. Today she had on a pair of snakeskin spike heels.

Usually it was fun to be around other

witches. Since one of the most important rules of the Witch Decree was No Telling, Claire and Luna had to be extremely secretive about even their smallest witch habits (like keeping one eye open when they sneezed or yawned). Grandy was always warning them that if their powers ever became known, the Decree Keepers up in Maine would snatch them away, pronto. So it was only in the company of other witches that the girls could feel truly comfortable.

But this weekend, the Fluffy problem was too distracting for Claire to feel too at ease.

After an early dinner served at the long cherrywood table in Grandy's dining room, the witches got down to business. They decided that, in order to save the Nature Preserve from developers, they would invoke a five-star spell. To Claire and Luna, the spell sounded complicated—all about hexing the topsoil so that it would be too rocky to break ground. There was lots of talk about soil components that was very boring for the twins.

With so much excited conversation, the girls were forgotten. Claire nibbled a crescent cookie that tasted too perfect. Secretly, she preferred her father's cooking, burns, spills, and all. Last weekend, he had made buckwheat pancakes with huckleberry syrup. And every time he flipped the pan, he said "*Voilà!*"

Soon he would be making pancakes in Texas. Saying "*Voilà!*" for Fluffy and Houston, his new family. Claire's eyes filled with tears, which she brushed away quickly, because the other witches could be nosy about why you were crying, and they always hoped it was about boys so they could get you to try out their latest love potions.

After dinner, she and Luna cleared the table and, because they were at Grandy's, they were allowed to perform a joint kitchen cleanup spell. Cleaning spells were almost as easy as repair spells. For this one, they held their hands crossed over the sink and chanted,

Everything dirty

And all that went stray—

Be washed, be dried,

And put away.

Dishes floated through the air and stacked themselves in the dishwasher. Counters were wiped; leftovers wrapped up and slid into the refrigerator as if by invisible hands. But that still left the jobs of sweeping the floor, which is actually a very hard spell, and sorting out the recycling, a modern spell still being test run up in Maine.

From the dining room came shouts and laughter.

"I don't think now is the time to bother Grandy with our Fluffy problem," said Claire as she put away the broom and dustpan.

"It's only seven o'clock. Maybe in an hour," agreed Luna.

So they went upstairs to Grandy's library and looked through her Big Book of Shadows. To get into the right mood, they dressed up in Grampy's velvet smoking jackets and hats, which were kept on hooks on the back of the library door. The girls had never known their

Grampy, who had been a nightclub singer and had disappeared mysteriously ten years ago. But Grandy and their mother missed him horribly.

"I think we would have liked him," said Luna. "At least, his clothes are very stylish."

When the clock struck eight, the coven was still downstairs, hooting and hollering, eating bonbons, and talking all about Old School. They were telling Miss Buzzard stories. Miss Buzzard had been their Old School Head. "Twice as charming as a werewolf, and half as attractive," Grandy liked to say about her.

The twins leaned over the banister and listened.

"Not now," said Claire.

"Maybe in an hour," agreed Luna.

When the girls crept downstairs at nine o'clock, Grandy was banging on the piano while Demeter, Isis, and Mikki sang three-part harmony to their favorite old show tunes.

"I've heard better voices from the seals at Seaworld!" Luna covered her ears.

"Daggers and druids, somebody stop them!" Claire covered her ears, too. "Let's check back in an hour."

But by ten o' clock, the coven had gathered in the kitchen to play poker.

"Aces are wild, and bedtime for twins!" Grandy yelled up the stairs.

"She's not even going to come up and tuck us in," said Claire as they folded Grampy's clothes and changed into their pajamas.

"What did I tell you?" Luna scoffed. "This was a bad time for us to visit. It's mid-month, and we weren't invited."

"We weren't *not* invited," answered Claire indignantly.

"Yes, but we weren't *especially* invited," said Luna.

"I don't see the difference," said Claire, who did, but hated to admit when she was wrong. "Anyway, we can ask what to do about Fluff tomorrow. We've still got plenty of time."

But the next morning, Grandy slept late and came down to breakfast with an ice pack over her eyes.

"I can't tie it on the way I used to," she grumbled. "If only your grandfather were around. He had a good cure for morning headaches. Something with seltzer water and salt. I can't remember. Oof, I'm hungry." She raised her pinkie and cast a quick breakfast spell.

Hens in the hen house,

Chickens on the loose.

Fry my eggs and pour my juice!

But Claire knew immediately she'd got the spell wrong (it's supposed to be *fox* on the loose) and Grandy was served a saucer of juice with a raw egg floating on top of it. The thing about those easy pinkie spells is that if one word is lost, a lot of mess is made.

Claire and Luna, who'd got up early to clean up last night's poker chips, piano music, and bonbon wrappers, sat very still and polite at the kitchen table. After Grandy had recast the spell and taken a few bites of fried egg, Claire could no longer wait. As they had planned, she began one sentence, then let Luna take the next, and so on.

"Grandy, a very horrible thing has happened to us."

"Dad is getting remarried."

"And Fluffy is from Texas, which is two thousand miles away."

"And we know she's going to want to move back there."

"Especially after she has Houston, because she'll want to raise him in the traditional Texan style."

"With dogies and spurs."

Claire took a deep breath. Here came the hard part, which Luna had been supposed to say—only she had lost her nerve and put in that unimportant piece about dogies and spurs instead. "And so, it behooves us to call on you, as Head Witch Arianna of Greater Bramblewine, to please help us with our trouble."

“Please, Grandy!” Luna implored. “We don’t want Dad to have a new family. We were first!”

Their grandmother pushed back in her chair and frowned so hard it was as if her whole face had sunk into her mouth.

A bad sign, thought Claire. She should have known. There had been plenty of warning. First, she and Luna had come to visit on the wrong weekend. Second, Grandy was not feeling well this morning. Third, Grandy had just miscast a spell, which usually made her think that she was losing her touch. The saying goes that powers wane as wisdom waxes, but when all was said and done, Grandy liked her witch power better than her witch smarts.

Now Grandy cracked her knuckles.

“Hear me out,” she began in her forceful Head Witch voice that could freeze a summer raindrop in midair. “The fury of the moment plays folly with the truth. Keep your wits, Luna and Claire, before you speak so strongly.” Then in her regular, Grandy voice, she said,

"Now who is this woman, this Fuzzy?"

"No, Fluffy. Fluffy Demarkle," Claire corrected. "She's a fashion editor. She eats mostly soy products. She's allergic to bees. She calls us 'sugar' and 'gals.' And she is our soon-to-be-stepmother who is stealing Dad off to Texas."

"Well, it's of no interest to me. If your father wants to marry a pygmy and move to—wherever pygmies live—then by all rights he should."

"If we could just learn a small spell, Grandy," Luna pleaded. "Nothing against Fluffy. Just a simple Keep-Dad-in-Philadelphia spell."

"Nonsense. Your father's life is not a game, and you girls know very well that No Destiny Changing is almost an important a rule as No Telling. That's all I have to say. If you need me, I'll be in the greenhouse." With that, Grandy stood up, collected her ice pack in one hand, Wilbur in the other, and stalked out the kitchen door.

"Grandy's sure in a bad mood. I guess we

could have waited until the right weekend." This was the closest Claire came to a you-told-me-so apology, and she was relieved when her sister decided to take it as one.

"What are we going to do now, Clairsie?" asked Luna gently.

Claire walked around the kitchen in a slow circle, her hands on her hips and her head tilted back.

"Methinks we will have to put this one in the brewing vats," she said. "And if Head Witch Arianna can't help us, then we shall take matters into our own hands. But for the meantime, we shall boycott Fluffy."

"Agreed," said Luna.

"Let's keep the boycott a secret from Justin. Because I think he likes old Fluff."

"Agreed," said Luna.

And they hooked pinkies on it.

3

The Pinkie-Spell Anti-Pulverizing Love Powder

"HAVE YOU NOTICED that Justin's been in a bad mood lately? I think he's in trouble," Luna mentioned one morning as the girls walked behind Justin to school. All three Bundkins went to Tower Hill Middle School, but while the twins were in fifth grade, Justin was two grades higher.

"Fluffy trouble?" asked Claire.

"I don't think so," said Luna. She

exchanged a frown with her sister. It had been over a week since Bad News Night, and neither she nor Claire had figured out a single way to stop their father from marrying Fluffy.

The problem was still brewing in the brewing vats.

Claire looked down the street. Even though Justin was supposed to walk next to them so they could all cross the lights together, he preferred to walk a block ahead. He said he was scouting for muggers, but the twins knew the real truth: a seventh grader didn't want to be seen walking with a couple of fifth graders, even ones who came from his own family.

"What kind of trouble, then?" asked Claire.

"Well, he's stayed inside the past two recesses."

"Ugh!" said Claire. Both girls hated indoor recess. "How do you know?"

"Because sometimes when I leave lunch early, I go watch him play that game, Destroyer, and he hasn't been playing all week. He's been in the library."

"Oooh, Destroyer!" exclaimed Claire. "I love-love-love that game."

"I hate-hate-hate that game," said Luna, who was terrible at all sports. "It hurts. I always get bopped on the head."

"Justin's great at Destroyer," said Claire. "Kids sometimes cheer when he plays it."

"Well, to get back to the point," continued Luna briskly, because she did not like to be reminded that both her brother *and* her sister were more athletic than she was, "at first, I also thought maybe Justin was mad about Dad and Fluff's engagement. But last night, he told me that Fluffy gave him her Dictaphone." Luna shook her head in disbelief. "He thinks she's a real princess."

"If Justin's in serious trouble, he'd never tell us," Claire said. "He thinks we're squirts."

"I know. That's why I was thinking how about we spy on him, like detectives?"

Spying on their brother was always an exciting idea, even if Justin wasn't in trouble. So the girls hung back, waiting for their brother to cross the next light. When he walked through Tower Hill's seventh-grade entrance, he was too far ahead to notice them following.

The seventh-grade hall looked different from the fifth-grade hall, thought Luna as they sneaked through it. It was more grown-up, especially since there were lockers in it. (Fifth and sixth graders kept their books in their desks.) Luna could not wait to be in seventh grade, when she would get her own locker. In fact, she already had cut out some magazine pictures of horses, and one of cleft-chinned Captain Xeno from *Galaxy Murk*, to decorate the inside of her future locker door.

When Justin got to his locker, he stopped and glanced around nervously. Then he hunched down and used his shirtsleeve to try to rub something off its surface. Finally, he gave up, grabbed his books, and slunk off to class.

The twins waited until he rounded the corner before they hurried over to his locker.

Scribbled in sloppy blue marker, they read:

Bundkin's my breakfast! S.Z.

"Who's S. Z.?" asked Claire.

"I don't know," Luna answered. "We'll have to do more detectiving."

Just then a couple of seventh-grade girls stopped at the locker next to Justin's. They read the locker scribble and started to laugh.

"Poor Justin," said one girl. "I hear Stew is going to *pulverize* him."

"Over what?" asked the other girl.

"Oh, who cares? Dumb guy-stuff." The girls giggled some more and then glided away like a pair of swans. Luna watched them go. Oh, she couldn't wait to be in seventh grade!

"Stew *Zumback*," she said, tracing her fingernail over the initials. "He's on the snow chain list. You know who he is, Clairsie. He's big and plays basketball and he has a little mustache that looks like his lip needs dusting."

"Anyone who wants to eat our brother for breakfast should be boycotted," Claire said sternly.

"The problem is, you plus me equals a whole lot less than Stew."

"I'm going to do something, anyhow!" Claire slammed her fist against Justin's locker. It made a crash of noise, and some seventh graders turned to look. "Whoever wants to eat my brother for breakfast has to answer to me first! I'm gonna confront him!"

"I wouldn't if I were you." But Luna was not Claire, and once her sister decided to do something, Luna could count on her to do it.

That afternoon, the twins spied Stew Zumback at the bus line. He was stuffing chips into his mouth as fast as he could before the line monitor caught him.

"Now let me do the talking." Claire grabbed Luna's hand and marched up. "Are you Stew Zumback?" she asked.

Stew turned, mid-chew, and frowned. "Who's asking?"

Claire's mouth snapped shut. Under Stew's beady eye, she seemed to have lost her nerve. Luna felt an odd and sudden surge of bravery.

She stepped forward in front of her sister.

"You keep away from our brother, Justin Bundkin," she squeaked. "Or one day, you might live to regret it."

Stew gaped, giving a full view of the potato chip paste inside his mouth.

"Get lost, twins," he said. "I'm gonna give Bundkin a black eye, just for your trouble. That kid's got it coming."

"We mean it!" squeaked Luna, after Claire still had not said a word.

Stew stepped closer. Luna saw that her height stopped at his armpit.

"And *I* mean, get lost!" he roared.

The twins ducked and ran.

"Now you've done it," huffed Claire. "A black eye! Poor Justin!"

"*I've* done it? *You* did it! You and your bad idea!"

"Was not!"

"Was, too!"

"At least I did the talking! At least I didn't just stand there!"

"So?" But Claire looked so embarrassed that Luna decided to drop it.

"Clairsie, I think that instead of looking for fights, from now on we should proceed with caution," said Luna. (To proceed with caution, in Luna's mind, was always the best way to proceed.) "Starting with going home and asking Justin *why* he's Stew Zumback's breakfast."

"Good idea!" Claire started to run down the street.

"Proceed with caution," Luna warned.

Claire took off like a shot. Luna trailed her all the way home, through the front door, and up the stairs to Justin's room.

"Justin-Justin-Justin! Why is Stew Zumback going to pulverize you? Why are you his breakfast, huh? Why-why-why?" shrieked Claire, taking a flying leap onto the middle of Justin's bed.

"Hey! Out of my room, squirt!" Justin ordered, looking up from his homework. But he didn't say it with his usual Justin energy. He didn't even make a grab for Claire, who, after finding his hacky sack under his pillow, began playing a lying-down version of the game.

Luna hovered in the doorway. "Is everything okay, Jus?" she asked.

"It's nothing. Stew wants to beat me up 'cause I slammed him out of Destroyer three times in one day," Justin mumbled. His face was red. "I can't help it if I'm awesome at that game. And Stew's an easy target. He's big, and he moves slow. I'd have a harder time hitting a parked car."

"Is that why you've been staying inside at recess?" Luna asked. "Is that why Stew wrote that stuff on your locker?"

"Yeah," Justin admitted. "The guy's just a jerk."

"Poor you, Justin," said Claire. "We tried to warn him off you today."

"You didn't have to do that. I can take care of myself," Justin answered stiffly. "I'm kind of known as a lone wolf around school, you know."

"You are *not*," Luna corrected. "You're hardly ever alone."

"Well, if you ever wanted to call me Lone Wolf, though, you could. It's kind of a nickname I've been working on."

"Okay," said Luna. She didn't want to point out that most nicknames were given by others, not self-started. Justin seemed depressed enough as it was.

"Are kids really talking about it?" he asked. "Jeez. Even in fifth grade." He looked sad. Then he looked grouchy. "Okay, squirts, you have five seconds left in my room before I start hollering. Four, three, two—"

The girls jumped out the door. Justin wasn't fun to be around once he decided to start hollering.

"If we really want to help Justin, there's only one solution," Luna said when they were safe in their room. She used her grave almost-one-star-witch voice. "We'll cast a spell."

"No!" Claire gulped. Casting spells without Grandy to supervise was almost as strong a rule as No Telling.

"Yes! A small spell. A harmless little

pinkie powder love spell," said Luna, who loved-loved-loved love spells. "A smushy, squishy, soften-up-Stew spell!"

Claire's brow puckered. "Last time we did a spell without Grandy, we made a big mistake, remember? We tried to get Mr. Nadeesh's cat out of a tree, and instead we turned it into a crow."

"That's because you said, 'unstick thy caw,' instead of 'claw.' Let me do the spell this time. Crumbs, Claire, we learned love powders years ago! Besides, they're harmless, you can even buy premade ones at some drugstores."

Luna looked at Claire. She knew that she and Claire were thinking the same thing. Sure, Justin could be obnoxious, but other times he was a terrific big brother who'd taught them how to do stomach-burps and headstands against the wall. If he needed witch protection, they ought to be gracious enough to give it. Otherwise, what was the point of witch powers?

They got to work.

Almost all the ingredients for the love powder could be found in the medicine chest or kitchen cupboard. The Little Book of Shadows called for talc, brown and white sugar, cinnamon, sweet basil, jasmine, and myrtle.

"I hope that the container is okay," said Claire. "It's supposed to be a cherished chalice. The only chalice I have is my Pooh drinking cup."

"As long as you're sure it's cherished," said Luna doubtfully. "It looks kind of chewed on the sides."

"This is my favorite cup!" exclaimed Claire. "It's perfect as it is!"

They pooled their allowances to get the jasmine and myrtle from the RiteAid, and they made the powder late that night, after Justin and their mother had gone to bed. At twelve minutes to midnight, they sneaked into his room, stood at the foot of his bed, crooked their right pinkies, and quickly chanted:

Goblet, chalice, cauldron, cup

Of love's ambition, fill 'er up!

Then they whispered Justin's name and Stew's name, sprinkled the powder over his outline, and tiptoed back to their room.

"If that does the trick, then it was worth losing sleep over," said Luna as they burrowed in their beds.

The next morning, Justin looked radiant. His eyes and skin seemed to glow. Even more strange, he walked in step with the twins to school and held their hands at the cross lights, the whole time whistling "You Are My Sunshine."

It was the handholding that made Luna think that maybe something in the spell had gone wrong. But what happened next was even more strange. After Justin dropped them off at the fifth-grade hall, the twins turned and followed Justin around the corner. They watched in dread as he strode right to where Stew and his buddies were leaning against the fire escape doors.

"I think you're the greatest person I ever

met!" Justin announced. He threw his arm around Stew's shoulder. The other guys started to laugh.

"You're crazy, Bundkin!"

"This some kinda joke?" growled Stew.

"Not at all. I have a very special feeling for you in my heart!"

"Get away from me!" barked Stew. "Or I'll give you a black eye!"

"You big lunk." Justin grinned. "That's a good one."

"Toenails and tombstones!" said Claire. She turned wide eyes on her twin. "What happened?"

"We mixed it up!" gasped Luna. "Justin's smushy for Stew! Where did we go wrong? Was it the chewed chalice?"

"Of course not!" Claire answered hotly.

That afternoon, back at home, Luna flipped open their Little Book of Shadows and reread. It turned out to be the smallest thing. They were supposed to say Stew's name first, then Justin's. In their excitement, they had done it the other way around. But of course the teeniest mistake can be devastating, even in a harmless pinkie powder spell.

"Grandy would pulverize us, if she ever found out!" Luna despaired.

"She'd never give us our stars and kittens," moaned Claire.

"How long 'til the spell wears off?"

Claire checked the book. "Three days! Poor Justin. I saw him hugging Stew at the fire drill. But I guess there's nothing to be done."

"There's one thing," Luna corrected. "We should be extra-extra nice to Justin. It's all our fault he's got two more days of slobbery Stew-chasing."

"Agreed," said Claire, and they hooked pinkies on it.

But that night at the dinner table, Justin surprised them.

"Hey, Mom, I guess it's just like you said—you really can kill people with kindness," he announced.

Their mother lowered her fork. "How's that?" she asked.

"I've had some problems with this kid at school, and I've been chasing him off by being extra nice. Like, every time I saw him today, I tackled him in a hug. By the end of the day, whenever he caught sight of me, he cleared out fast in the opposite direction! Problem solved!"

Jill Bundkin shook her head and laughed. "Well, that's one way of taking my advice," she said.

"I guess we shouldn't have pinkie-hooked to be extra-extra nice," said Claire. But since there was no going back on a pinkie hook, Luna gave Justin full rights to the remote control, while Claire took out the trash even though it was Justin's turn.

They even served him the last of the carton of Schmidt's coffee ice cream when there wasn't enough to split three ways.

"Is this Be Kind to Big Brothers week?" asked their mother. Being a doctor, she was watchful of sudden changes.

"Love comes around and goes around," Claire answered.

"And," added Luna, "it's never too late to change your mind about your brother."

4
Fluffy's Dresses

UNAWARE THAT SHE had been boycotted, Fluffy set the day of the wedding for June fifth.

"Mark that date!" she told the twins over the phone.

On their wall calendar, Claire marked a square black border around June fifth. Inside the square, she drew in a picture of Fluffy with crossed eyes and fangs and a

Texas hat and the word yuck! underneath. (Since Claire was terrible at drawing, the picture was extra ugly, which made it extra good.)

Boycotting Fluffy was the only plan, unfortunately, that had popped out of the twins' brewing vats. And all it meant really was thinking of new excuses for not spending weekends with their dad.

For example, they skipped one weekend by deciding to attend Julie Aledort's indoor swimming party instead.

"I thought you girls hated swimming parties," said their mother, which was true, but only because witches are known to hate-hate-hate still water, the kind that is in lakes and pools. (Ocean water is a different story. Since it's controlled by moon tides, witches enjoy it enormously.)

And the twins had a terrible time at Julie's since all they could do was watch everyone else get wet and have fun.

But at least they didn't have to see Fluffy.

The following week crossed into April, so that weekend they went out to Bramblewine.

"But you were out there two weekends ago," said their mother.

"Yes, but we *always* go the first weekend of the month," said Claire. "You can't go against *tradition.*"

"I'm sure your father misses you," said their mother.

The twins missed him, too.

"Nobody said boycotting would be easy," Claire reminded Luna.

Luckily, April was Claire's favorite month at Bramblewine. New grass was starting to come up, and Grandy was devoting every hour to her spring plantings. (Witches tend to be passionate about their gardens.)

"Are you girls over your snit with Woolly?" asked Grandy, as the three of them were planting pea squash in Grandy's organic vegetable patch.

"Fluffy," Luna corrected. "She's awful."

"In what way?" asked Grandy.

"In *every* way," said Claire, though at that moment, she couldn't think of any particular way.

"Silly grudges will never get you your first star," Grandy warned. "The GSTs are hard enough without soaking yourselves in negative energy."

The twins looked up from their planting. "GSTs?" they asked together.

"Girls, I'm sure I've told you about GSTs. It's the National Witches' Bureau one-star test. It's divided into three parts. You must do something good, something smart, and something tricky."

Of course, Grandy never had told them about the GSTs. Grandy's way of teaching was very sneaky, and the girls knew better than to ask. After she went up to the house, they were able to speak privately.

"Grandy must think we're ready for our stars, or she never would have mentioned those GSTs," said Luna. "Imagine us finally as one-star witches!"

"We'd get our kittens," said Claire, who had been wanting her witch-kitten ever since she could remember.

All that day and the next, they waited and hoped Grandy would tell them more about the GSTs. Instead, she made them help her put up her tomato frame, and they spent the rest of the weekend painting a coat of weather-proof sealant on the porch steps.

There came one final false hope when Grandy dropped them off at the train.

"Here, this is something very important!" she said, thrusting a box into Claire's eager arms.

"A GST study guide?" breathed Luna.

"Our kittens!" exclaimed Claire.

But it turned out to be some purple-print pajamas for their mother.

"Mom means well," said Jill Bundkin, after the twins got home and she opened the gift, "but these are outrageous." And she packed the pajamas straight into her MOM—CRAZY STUFF box that she kept under her bed.

"I guess we'll just have to keep patient,"

said Claire. She hadn't *really* thought there would be kittens in the box, but it was pretty disappointing to see pajamas.

Meantime, the boycotting began to get difficult.

"I hope you girls will see us next weekend," said Fluffy when she and their dad dropped off Justin that Sunday.

"We'll go horseback riding. And I cleaned the grill for a cookout," said their dad.

"Actually, we volunteered for Philadelphia Cares weekend cleanup project," said Claire.

"Claire and I need to refresh our commitment to community service," said Luna, quoting the flier. Their father gave them both a funny look.

"Can't argue with that" was all he said.

The cleanup turned out to be a pretty good experience. Their mother and Steve came along, and afterward they went to The Aubergine, where Steve made them fancy cheese omelets.

"Steve is a way lot easier to get along with than Fluff," Luna decided.

"Well, Fluff was okay, too, until she wanted to marry Dad," Claire said. "It's one thing to *borrow* a mom or dad. It's another thing to *steal* them off to Texas."

"The problem with boycotting Fluff is that we have to boycott Dad, too," said Luna. "And I don't think he's too happy about that."

He wasn't.

"I miss my twins," he told them on Sunday, when he came by to drop off Justin. The twins jumped in the backseat to talk for a little while.

"Where's Fluffy?" asked Claire.

"Right this minute, she's waiting for me at the airport. She was in Texas visiting her family," their father told them.

"Aha!" said Claire.

"Aha what?" asked their father.

"Just aha!" said Claire.

Louis Bundkin shifted around in the driver's seat and looked perplexedly at his daughters. "One reason I wanted to spend this weekend with you girls was because I want to be sure you felt comfortable about getting a stepmother," he said. "You know that nothing has changed in my feelings toward you kids. You're my top priority, no matter what."

"Of course we feel comfortable," said Claire, although just then her throat felt tight. "Besides, all stepmothers are wicked."

"Fluffy's not wicked," said their dad. Then, in his reporter's voice, he asked, "Who said she was wicked? Why would anyone say she was wicked? What would make you think she was wicked?"

"No, Dad, in fairy tales, Claire meant. Not in real life," said Luna, with an elbow-jab for Claire.

"I think he's figured out about the boycott," Luna said after they got out of the car and watched him drive away.

"I hope so," said Claire. She was getting tired of their dad not knowing how they were feeling.

That night, the phone rang. It was Fluffy. First she spoke to their mother, who mostly said "uh-huh" and "I see" and "that's true." Then she signaled for the girls to get on. So Luna picked up the kitchen phone while Claire took the line in the living room.

"I'd like you take you gals shopping for your bridesmaid dresses tomorrow, if you aren't busy," said Fluffy. "Your mom says you're free tomorrow after school. We'll go to Regent's. Is that peachy by you-all?"

It was a bad idea to be in different rooms. Claire couldn't tell what Luna was thinking.

"Okay," they both said in small voices.

"Great!" Fluffy exclaimed. "Then we'll have tea on the top floor. Do you know there's a teahouse on the top floor of Regent's? And it's called Top Floor! Funny, huh?"

Neither twin said a word.

"See you at three-fifteen," said Fluffy, more quietly. "And I promise it'll be fun. Bye for now, gals."

"Funny, huh!" yelled Claire in a Texas

voice after they hung up their phones. "Bye for now, gals!" It felt good to make fun of Fluffy's Texas voice. It felt good to make fun of Fluffy, period.

Luna laughed.

"Alone with Fluffy," said Claire, walking in a circle and rubbing her hands together. "Wouldn't it be fun to put a little spell on her?"

Luna bit her lip. "No spells," she said worriedly. "Not after the mess-up with Justin's love powder."

"A teensy little spellsie," argued Claire, who did not mind making mistakes as much as her sister.

"No spells," Luna insisted. "Until we have a plan, anything to do with Dad and Fluff should be done with our regular human brainpower. Any other way is just too dangerous."

But when Fluffy came to pick them up at Tower Hill Middle School the next afternoon, the only regular human-brain-powered plan the twins had come up with was to act bored.

"Are you gals excited?" asked Fluffy, not noticing their boredom. "I just looove shopping. It really revs my engine!" She was all dressed up in a sparkle-studded blouse and matching pants. She looked very flashy, Claire decided. She hoped nobody at school mistook Fluffy for their real mother. Yuck.

"So how did you get the name Fluffy?" asked Claire on the way out to Regent's. She tried to make her voice bored.

"I'm the youngest of five sisters, and they all liked to style my hair," Fluffy explained. "So anyone could always spot me in a crowd 'cause I was the one with the fluffiest hair! Funny, huh?"

"Then what's your real name?" asked Luna.

"Sugar, it's nothing to wish for." Fluffy lowered her voice. "It's Edith Hortense. I was named after both my grandmas. My mama and daddy used up four names on my sisters before they ran out of excuses and named me after both their mothers. Two stones for one bird, my daddy liked to say!"

"It's not so bad," Claire lied. Inside, she gagged. Edith Hortense! Claire loved beautiful, interesting words, and she could not get hold of *anything* beautiful in the sound of Edith Hortense. It was a name so bad it almost had a taste of avocado in it.

For a minute, Claire felt sorry for Fluffy.

She forgot about all that as soon as they got to Regent's.

Regent's was a fantastic department store. For one thing, it gave out tons of free samples. By the time they got to the fourth floor, Missy Dresses, Claire and Luna had filled their coat pockets with free aloe-infused tissues, chocolate and butterscotch candies, lavender hand lotion, and one bottle of opal nail polish apiece. Fluffy let them take the escalators, so they didn't miss a single freebie.

"So many dresses," said Fluffy as they entered the Missy Dresses section. "Ooh, look at this cantaloupe-colored one! Ooh, or the linen."

The girls split up into different aisles. In

spite of their "act bored" rule, Claire saw that her sister liked looking at all the dresses. Ugh—she didn't! Her boredom was real. Claire picked up a soft blue flowered dress and held it against herself. Then held up a pale green one.

Bo-ring!

Fluffy was pretending to inspect some shoes, but her eyes studied Claire carefully.

"You look as pretty as a picture in seafoam green," she blurted. "My best friend Denise's favorite color is seafoam. She's a real cut-up, Denise. She's got twin boys, five years old now. I hope you can meet her, she lives on a ranch. And you know, my parents have already offered you gals a place to stay with them. There's more than enough room."

Hearing Fluffy say this, Claire scowled and hooked the dress back on the rack. Texas! Twins! Ranch! Fluffy's parents! Her eyes narrowed. She felt a prickliness come over her. She did not want to go to Texas, to meet somebody else's twins! And she did not like the idea that Fluffy's best friend lived in Texas!

"Texas is very far away," Claire mentioned.

"Naw. It's just a hop, sugar," said Fluffy, with a wink.

"So, would you ever move back there? Permanently, I mean?"

"Oh, I don't know," said Fluffy. "I don't give it too much thought, these days. Too much else going on."

Claire's scowl deepened. Luna had been right all along. Fluffy really was planning to run off to Houston. Her friends were there. Her family was there. And someday soon, their dad would be there, too.

Claire watched as Luna browsed happily around the racks of dresses, selecting one thing and then pursing her lips and putting it back. Luna wasn't even pretending to act bored anymore. She'd forgotten.

Slowly, a plan formed in Claire's mind. She took a few steps back and surveyed the entire Missy Dresses selection. She waited for the right color to catch her eye.

Pea-soup green.

Sickly pink.

Muddy-water brown.

Black and yellow.

Black and yellow! Yuck! She ran to it.

It might have been the ugliest dress in the store. Black and yellow bumblebee stripes, with puffy sleeves and two fat bows, a yellow one in the front and a black one in the back.

"Gorgeous!" Claire cried, pulling it off the rack. Fluffy hurried to see.

"You found one—oh, no!" Fluffy jumped back from the dress, swatting at it with her hand as if it really were a giant bumblebee. Luna looked over. Seeing the dress, a smile slowly spread over her face.

"Oh, yes!" Luna squealed, hopping to her side. "Claire, you are a genius!"

"Are you—are you positive?" Fluffy reached forward carefully, as if the dress might sting her. She rubbed the fabric between her fingers. It made a slithering, oily sound.

"Positive!" said Claire. "This is the most perfect dress I have ever seen! Oh, gosh, if I don't get to wear this dress at your wedding, Fluffy, I'll be crushed! It's so gorgeous. Say you like it!"

"Say you like it, Fluffy!" Luna began to jump up and down. Now both girls were squealing.

"I . . . it's not my taste," Fluffy answered. "And you gals know how I'm allergic to bees and all, so those particular colors don't . . ." Fluffy touched her hand to her forehead. "Oh, my," she said. "I think I'm swelling up."

The girls looked at her. It was true. Fluffy's cheeks and chin were beginning to puff like balloons. When she stuck out her hands, her fingers were thick as cigars, her wristwatch squeezed on tight as an elastic band.

"It's like I really got bee stung," Fluffy groaned.

"It'll pass," said Claire. That's what her mother always said whenever she had a cold or flu.

"Oh, my." Fluffy touched her plump fingers

to her bulging cheeks. "I just need to calm down. A psychological reaction. Funny, huh?" But she didn't sound as if she found it too funny.

"We can still get the dresses, right, Fluffy?" asked Claire.

Fluffy blinked. For the second time that day, Claire felt sorry for her. She tried to push it away, and instead she pictured her dad in a Texas hat, teaching little Houston how to make buckwheat pancakes with huckleberry sauce.

Then Fluffy seemed to decide something. Her mouth zippered into a line. She patted her puffy cheeks and she smoothed down the front of her sparkle-studded blouse.

"Any dress you wanted, that's what I said. I'm just having a temporary adverse reaction, sugar. Let's go find a seamstress," she said. She took another step back from the bumblebee dress. "You-all will probably need to have these fitted."

"Bzz bzz bzz!" said Luna in Claire's ear. "Good thinking, Clairsie."

Claire grinned.

After the fitting, Fluffy decided there was not enough time to go to the Top Floor for tea. The drive back to 22 Locust Street was silent and speedy. Fluffy even ran a yellow light, she seemed so anxious to get the girls home.

She gave a weary half-wave when she dropped them off.

"How was it?" asked their mother when she opened the door.

"Great!" they chorused.

"Oh, I'm glad. To tell you the truth, your dad and I were worried that you girls were going through a little trouble adjusting to the engagement."

"Not at all. Fluffy's a real honey," said Luna.

"She's just the bee's knees," Claire added.

Then she followed Luna up the stairs and into their room, where they flung themselves on their beds and laughed into their pillows.

"But you know, Loon, even a dress that brings on an allergic reaction doesn't mean the wedding's off," Claire said, after they had recovered. "We could still end up with a step-Fluffy."

"Next time, we need a plan, not a trick," agreed Luna.

"Or a spell," said Claire. "Maybe getting rid of Fluffy is part of our GST test. As something good, something smart, and something tricky."

"That's a very intelligent point, Clairsie," said Luna. "When you talk like that, you definitely don't seem a whole thirteen minutes younger."

5
Luna Alone

THROUGHOUT MOST of their fifth-grade year at Tower Hill Middle School, Mrs. Sanchez had been the twins' teacher. They loved-loved-loved her.

In fact, even before they met her, the twins loved-loved-loved Mrs. Sanchez. That was because Justin always used to tell them Mrs. Sanchez stories. "Mrs. Sanchez never yells. She wears perfume that smells like oranges. She plays music during art and free time. And if you want to go back to Five A to visit her every once in a while, she doesn't make you feel babyish about it. She was basically the coolest teacher I ever had."

So Luna had been excited, back in September, when she and Claire had both gotten assigned to 5A. That was Mrs. Sanchez's room! Although 5A would rotate some classes with Mr. Rosenthal's 5B, getting 5A officially meant they belonged to Mrs. Sanchez.

"You lucked out," Justin told them. "Besides, Rosenthal's got hair in his ears and moss on his teeth, and sometimes he smells like sour milk."

Not Mrs. Sanchez. "Welcome, this year's beloved Five A kids," Mrs. Sanchez told them that very first day. "Let me step back and get a look at you. I see we have twins! Now *that* is a good-luck charm!"

Luna smiled across the aisle at Claire, who smiled back. It was nice to be singled out as a good-luck charm.

And Justin was right. Mrs. Sanchez was the best teacher, ever. She showed them how to make dream catchers, she hummed under her breath, and she took them on a field trip every week.

"Philadelphia is one of the greatest cities in the world," she said. "Let's get to know it!"

Then, in October, Mrs. Sanchez had made a surprise announcement. She stood in front of the class with a big smile on her face. "My husband and I are expecting a child next year, in mid-April. I will be able to teach all the way up until then, and afterward I am taking off the rest of the year to be at home with our new baby. But I'm happy to tell you that Tower Hill Middle school already has found a wonderful substitute teacher to finish off the year with you. Her name is Ms. Fleegerman, and she used to live in Hawaii."

The twins exchanged unhappy faces with all the other kids in the classroom, because Mrs. Sanchez was everybody's favorite teacher, and nobody wanted a new one.

And even before they had met her, the twins knew they would hate-hate-hate old Ms. Fleegerman.

Luckily, "sometime next year in the middle of April" was months ahead, and pretty soon the class forgot about Mrs. Sanchez's baby.

"That's because she wasn't having a baby the usual way," declared Claire. "If Mrs. Sanchez had been pregnant, then at least we would have had a reminder every day."

"Like a Fleegerman countdown," added Luna.

So it came as a surprise, on the second Monday of April, when the twins walked into 5A and saw a strange woman sitting at Mrs. Sanchez's desk.

"Aloha, class," she said. "My name is Ms. Fleegerman. I am happy to give you some very good news. Over the weekend, Louisa and Randy Sanchez became proud parents of an eight-pound baby girl. At the end of the day, we will make congratulations cards."

The room was in a rumble of confusion.

For one thing, a few kids did not know what "aloha" meant. (It is Hawaiian for hello and good-bye.) Second, it took a minute to realize that Louisa and Randy Sanchez meant Mrs. Sanchez and some husband nobody had ever met. And third, everyone had sort of forgotten about how Mrs. Sanchez and her husband had been planning to adopt a baby.

The final thing was that Ms. Fleegerman was very strange looking. She was tall as a lamppost and skinny as a needle, with hair that looked as it had been chewed off instead of cut. She wore blue-framed glasses and orange nylon stockings. Worst of all, when she saw the twins, her face scrunched up as if she'd swallowed a sourball.

"Why weren't you twins split up into different rooms?" she asked. "That's no way to assert your individuality."

"We assert our individuality together," said Claire, and a few kids grinned because Claire was known to be sort of wise.

Ms. Fleegerman made a hen-clucking sound in her throat, then wrote something down in her teacher's notebook. Something bad, Luna knew.

"Old Ms. Fleegerman is even meaner than we expected," said Luna that night at dinner. Steve was over, and he had made a special chef's dinner. Chicken pâté to start. Then lamb Provençal and potatoes au gratin, then individual crème brulées. Steve's dinners were a mouthful to speak, but were also good to eat (though not as good as Licks 'n' Sticks).

"What did she do?" asked Justin.

"Nothing yet. But it'll happen, mark my words."

"Luna, you are a doomsday prophet," said their mother. "Be fair. Give old Ms. Fleegerman a chance."

"How old is she, anyway?" asked Steve.

"Somewhere between thirty and fifty-two," guessed Luna. "Old."

"Let me know when she does something mean," said their mother. "So far, you have no proof in your pudding."

Luna did not need proof or a pudding to know.

Sure enough, the very next morning, something mean had happened. When the girls walked into 5A, Claire's desk was missing.

"Where could it have gone?" asked Claire. She jumped down on her hands and knees and began scrambling around. "Here, desk-y desk! Here, desk!"

The other kids started laughing. Jemina Consolo dropped to her hands and knees, too.

"Here, desk. Come here, girl!"

"What's going on in here? What are you doing on the floor?" Suddenly, Ms. Fleegerman stood in the doorway. "Oh, yes. Claire Bundkin, you will find your desk in Mr. Rosenthal's class, in Five B. I spoke with Mrs. Hass, and she agreed to separate you two." She walked over to the girls and put a hand on each of their shoulders. "Don't worry, this is a good idea. Studies of identical twins prove that it is important for them to maintain separate classroom identities." She spoke as if she were talking out of a book.

Luna looked at Claire and Claire looked at Luna. Never in their school-day lives had they ever, ever been separated. Not even preschool. In preschool, they had even shared a cubby and napped on the same mat.

But Mrs. Hass was the school principal. There was not much a person could do, once something was agreed to by Mrs. Hass. Very sneaky of Ms. Fleegerman, thought Luna, to get Mrs. Hass on her side.

"Bye!" said Claire. "See you at lunch!" Claire got upset in a different way from Luna. Her face turned red, like their dad's. And she seemed to get very pointy all over, as if a thousand porcupine quills were poking off the surface of her skin. Now, even though she was smiling, she looked pointy as a sword.

She slammed the door to 5A so hard that the floor trembled.

Luna drooped. She went to her desk. She looked across the aisle. Instead of Claire, she saw Adam Chow. Adam was Luna's cleanup partner and could copy any drawing perfectly.

Luna really liked him, but he wasn't Claire.

Luna's way of getting upset was to crawl back into the smallest corner of herself, and that's what she did. She could not pay a second of attention to concepts in math, or reading comprehension, or science. In fact, if the school started to sink into the ground, Luna might not have noticed.

All she knew was that Claire was gone, and she hated it.

In computer lab, which 5A and 5B took together, only at different ends of the lab, Luna sent Claire an e-spell. An e-spell is just like e-mail, only it's magic. It was one of the few spells Grandy allowed the girls to cast unsupervised. Most hackers can do it without magic, anyway. An e-spell is like a regular e-mail, only written in invisible computer pixel so that nobody except the receiver can read it. Luna's e-spell went like this:

Dear Clairsie,
I'm so miserable I could die. Who
does Fleegermonster think she is,

switching you out of 5A? Tonight
let's ask Mom if we can change
schools. I wouldn't mind going to
Overbrook Middle. I heard they
sometimes have eggrolls for lunch.
Love, Luna

A few minutes later, her e-spell reply came in.

Loooon, if we change schools now we
miss mayfair & book fair & the lady
who's coming next week w/ her pet
trick monkeys. u r the lucky one—i
got rosenthal all day & he smells
like sower milk!!!!!!

It was not the reply Luna had expected.

"You are staring very intently at that blank screen, Luna Bundkin." Ms. Fleegerman's voice barked loud behind her. "I wish you would focus as hard on the assignment at hand. Please insert your CD-ROM and download the 'fun with fractions' file."

After computer lab, 5A and 5B rotated. In the hallway, Claire waved and made a sad face. Luna made a sad face back, but Claire did not see it because now she was whispering with Xander Wessels, the new kid whom Claire once said was a jerk. Claire must have decided he was not such a jerk, after all.

The day went from miserable to devastating. At lunch, Luna sat with Adam Chow, and in music appreciation, she stood between Frieda Gunderson and Helen Polinski. She realized that she didn't know Adam, Frieda, or Helen very well at all, although all three of them had come to the twins' last birthday party. Luna was so used to having Claire at her side that it had never seemed important to make friends with other people in their grade.

First no Mrs. Sanchez, now no Claire. It was that horrible old Ms. Fleegerman's fault. Luna closed her eyes and imagined all the spells she would cast on Ms. Fleegerman once she took her GSTs and became a one-star witch. She would cast the Twisted-Toes and Toads spell. The Erase-Facecream spell. The Expanding Wart-Picker's spell. Thinking of all the good spells made her laugh out loud.

Ms. Fleegerman glared. "Is there something so amusing about chorus, Miss Bundkin, that you would like to share it with us?"

"No, thanks, Ms. Fleegerman."

She could feel the whole class staring. How embarrassing! With no Claire on her side, and Ms. Fleegerman singling her out, Luna sensed that the other kids of 5A were beginning to view her differently. Maybe they were thinking that she was dumb twin, or the weird twin. The not-as-good-as-the-other twin.

It was awful.

"How was your first day in Five B?" she asked Claire as they walked home together.

"Not as bad as I thought. Alexa and Courtney and I made up a club. We named it the Mariposa Club, because butterflies are our club symbol, and *mariposa* is the Spanish word for butterfly. Isn't that a great word? Courtney even markered a mariposa on the bathroom stall door. You can be in our club, too, if you want. And look!" Claire rolled up her arm to show the pink-and-purple butterfly just above her elbow. "Alexa drew that on me. Doesn't it look just like a real tattoo?"

"Not really," Luna answered. She could hardly even talk from sadness.

"How's old Ms. F? Luckily, I only have to see her for natural history class and computer sciences."

"Gee, thanks for rubbing it in," said Luna.

At home, Luna dragged herself upstairs to their mother's room and closed the door. Their mother's room was very peaceful. It had a feather comforter and scented candles and many framed pictures of Justin, Luna, and Claire. But right now, Luna did not want to look at any pictures of herself. She turned them all facedown. Then she spied one of her mother's fuzzy slippers on the floor. It looked a little bit like a kitten.

Luna picked up the slipper, stretched out on the bed, and pulled the comforter up to her neck. She hugged the slipper, wishing that she had a real little kitten for a lonely time like now. She let a tear plop onto the pillow. And another. She closed her eyes.

"Luna?"

Luna's eyes opened. The room had gone dark. Her mother was sitting next to her on the bed. "Are you all right?" Her hand was cool against Luna's forehead. "You don't feel feverish. Is that my slipper you're holding?"

"Sorry, Mom. I'm okay. I didn't mean to fall asleep in here." The pillow smelled spitty. Luna raised her head, handed over the slipper, and wiped her cheek.

"Is there anything you want to talk about?" Now her mother reached over to the bedside table and stood one of the pictures upright. Luna looked hard at the photograph, taken at the beach after she and Justin and Claire had spent the entire afternoon digging a hole. She and Claire were standing in the hole on either side of Justin, so the picture was of Justin's entire face but only the tops of the twins' heads to their noses. It was almost impossible to know that Luna was the twin on the right.

Seeing the picture made Luna's eyes fill up again. "Claire got moved into Five B," she said.

"I know. She told me. She said that apart from missing you, it wasn't as bad as she expected."

Luna sniffled, then put her face in her hands. "When we're apart, Claire gets to keep her whole self, but I'm only half of me."

"Oh, Luna!" Her mother hugged her very long. Then she said, "Let me tell you a story. When you and Claire were little, nobody could tell you apart except for your dad and I. Do you know how? Because Claire was awake all day, and you were awake all night." She smiled to herself, remembering. "So we always knew you from Claire, because Claire shone with the sun and you shone with the moon."

"But we don't go to school at night!" Luna wailed.

Her mother smoothed back Luna's hair. "What I mean to say is, you both shine in different phases. Wait until the glare wears off this change and you feel more comfortable with it.

Then you'll shine, too, in your own special light."

"What if I don't shine?"

Her mother's eyes narrowed in thought and then she spoke seriously. "If you *really* feel that you need to be with Claire, then I'll have a talk with Ms. Fleegerman. As far as I'm concerned, children don't need to switch rooms midyear for their own or anyone else's good. But will you promise to think of it as a challenge, and give it a try?"

Luna nodded, although the only thing she wanted to try was to put Claire's desk, and everything else, back to the way it was.

The next day was just as lonely, though, and so was the next. Claire, however, was going to a Friday-night pizza party with other members of the Mariposa Club.

"You can come, too, of course, Loon," she said, but Luna said no thanks. She didn't know Alexa and Courtney that well.

By the middle of the next week, Luna was wondering when her mother was going to have that talk with old Ms. Fleegerman.

Recess was especially lonely. She had used to have recess with Claire, but now she always took a book to read on the tires. Today she had forgotten to bring out a book. Some of the other kids were playing Destroyer, and a few were doing gymnastics. Luna was not good at either of those things.

When Claire had been around, they had used to do gymnastics, too, with Luna spotting for Claire and then scoring her from one to ten. Without Claire, Luna realized that she didn't love-love-love gymnastics so much, after all. In fact, without Claire, Luna wouldn't have minded indoor recess.

Luna sat on the tires and kicked her legs. Then she walked out to the blacktop to watch kids get slammed out of Destroyer. After a few minutes, she picked up a rock and started to draw on the blacktop. It was a good rock, with a sharp part for details and a blunt part for shading.

First she drew Grandy's cat, Wilbur. She drew him sitting in the branches of a shaggy cypress tree. After a few minutes, some of the kids who had been slammed out of Destroyer began to creep and then to clump around her, watching.

"Hey, look what she drew!"

Behind the tree, Luna drew a sliver of moon. She shaded in some clouds.

"That's really good, Luna." Some of the gymnasts had stopped their front flips and back flips to watch.

Soon almost a dozen kids, including Mr. Dooley, the recess monitor, had made a giant circle around her.

"I didn't even know you could draw, Luna," said Adam Chow. "Why aren't you helping us with the scenery for our play?"

Luna shrugged. Claire was awful at drawing, so they both had signed up for stage-managing.

"Think about it," said Adam. "I'm sure it's not too late."

"Okay," said Luna.

"I saw your nice drawing at Five B recess,"

said Claire that afternoon as they walked home from school. "Now Courtney and Alexa really want you to be in our club. You'd draw the best mariposas of all. All you have to do to join is hold your breath for one minute and eat a handful of grass. Think about it."

"Okay," said Luna.

After a couple of days of thinking about it, Luna decided not to be in the Mariposa Club. Instead, she switched over from stage-managing to painting the play scenery with Adam Chow. The play that year was *The Princess and the Pea.*

"It's mostly drawing palaces and forests," said Adam.

But palaces and forests were Luna's specialty. And she noticed that every time she picked up her paintbrush, other kids put theirs down to watch.

Soon she was giving them tips. "If you use a lot of water, then you can always go back for a do-over." Or, "Sometimes a dot of white here and there can make a surface look shiny."

One afternoon, during A and B's hall rotation, Luna found herself in a debate about whether *The Princess and the Pea* was a girl play or a boy play or both. Adam Chow was on Luna's side (they thought it was both) and Jeb Myers disagreed (he said it was a girl play), but it was a good kind of argument. Luna was surprised that she had so much strong opinion inside her. She felt for a minute like one of Grandy's buddies. It took a nudge from Adam to look across the hall.

Claire was waving to her.

Luna waved back.

"You don't have to have that talk with old Ms. Fleegerman," Luna said that night to her mother when she came in to kiss the twins good-night.

"Have things become a little easier for you?" asked her mother.

Luna thought for a minute. "Let's just say, I think I'm phasing into it," she answered.

6

Aloha Means Hello and Good-bye

"MOM, ARE YOU sad about Fluffy?" asked Claire.

She and Luna and Justin were all sitting in the living room, trying to help their mother close her suitcase. She was leaving for Arizona to speak at a medical convention. She would be away until late the next night. "Long after all you munchkins are in bed," she told them.

"Now why would you ask a thing like

that?" Jill Bundkin raked her hands through her hair so that it spiked like a cactus. "I have an idea. Girls, sit on the suitcase. Justin, you push down from one side, and I'll push from the other."

The twins sat. Justin and their mother pushed.

The suitcase would not close.

"Just because," Claire continued, "if you and Dad were still married, then he would be going with you to Arizona for company."

"Girls, off. Let's flip the suitcase." The twins got off. They flipped the suitcase. "One of the interesting things about divorce," said Jill Bundkin, "is that it makes a person independent." She sat down hard on the suitcase. It still would not close. "Besides, I don't mind going to Arizona alone. I'm looking forward to it, actually. The air is thin and easy on my sinuses."

"And Mom could always take Steve, stupid," said Justin. "She wants to be a lone wolf on this trip." He let out a fantastic wolf howl.

The twins covered their ears.

"Justin," said their mother, "don't call your sister stupid. Anyway, Claire, to answer your question, no, I'm not sad about Fluffy. I am happy with Steve and your dad is happy with Fluffy. In my opinion, she seems like a levelheaded woman, in spite of her name."

"I like her, too. She gave me a disposable camera, last time I was over," said Justin. "She's always getting cool stuff from her job."

"Hey, we didn't get any camera," said Luna.

"That's because you never go there, stupid."

"Don't call your sister stupid," said their mother. "Now, watch this!" She gave a backward leap into the air, then landed hard on the suitcase. The locks snapped into place.

Everybody applauded, then Justin picked up the suitcase and hauled it to the door.

"You girls need to find a way to build an understanding with Fluffy," said their mother, pinching each of their noses. "But right now, I'm more concerned you understand that Grandy is the boss while I'm gone. Okay, pile on the kisses and hugs, because I won't see you for two whole days!"

They attacked, even Justin, who acted more like himself when nobody from school was around to see him.

Outside, a checkered cab pulled up with a beep, and everyone watched through the window as Grandy and Wilbur leaped out. In one hand, Grandy held her flowered overnight bag; in the other, she grasped a dragon-handled walking cane. (The cane was not magic. It was meant to shoo pigeons.)

"Mom, hold that cab!" shouted their mother as the cabby drove off. "Oh, rats! I really needed that ride to the airport!"

Then Grandy crooked a pinkie and cast:

Back, back

A seven-second tack.

It was a time-rewind spell, and now they all were hugging their mother good-bye again, and outside they heard Grandy saying to the cabby, "Wait here for my daughter. She's going to the airport."

Being witches, only the twins (and Grandy) felt the time rewind.

They followed their mother as she bumped her suitcase down the steps.

"Gosh, Mom, that cat looks just like all your others." Jill Bundkin leaned down. She studied Wilbur with her serious, doctor-diagnosing face. "He must be in the same ancestral line."

"Of course," said Grandy. "This is Wilbur the Fifth."

Wilbur closed one eye and yawned. Only a witch cat can do that. (All other, regular cats have to close both eyes when yawning.)

Their mother wrinkled her nose. "If I didn't know that it was impossible, I'd say you had the same exact ugly old Wilbur that I remember from my childhood. Right down to the same raggedy right ear."

Wilbur sniffed. Since he was a witch cat, he could understand humanspeak and he did not like to be insulted. He was also sensitive about his ear.

"You'd better get along, sweetie," said Grandy, giving her daughter a little nudge.

In Claire's opinion, Grandy had never been much fun to have as a baby-sitter. She did not cast any spells (unless it was an emergency), she checked napkins for hidden vegetables, and she did not even let them stay up late.

"Your mother's house, your mother's rules," she always said.

While she had stayed over many times, it was always for one night or over the weekend, and it was always the same.

Bo-ring!

Which made it extra surprising the next morning when Claire stumbled out to the kitchen, last to breakfast as usual, and found Grandy sitting at the table all dressed up in her black suit and silver star earrings and holding a potted orchid.

"Where are you going?" she asked as she sat down and grabbed the Lucky Oats from Justin before he polished off the box.

"To school with you children of course. What else am I supposed to do?"

"But grandparents don't go to school," said Claire.

"Do I look like 'grandparents' to you?" snapped Grandy, making quote marks with her fingers.

"Mmmnnn," said Claire, who thought that Grandy looked pretty much exactly like "grandparents."

"I always walk a block ahead to check for muggers, so good-bye." Justin jumped up, grabbed his bag lunch, and ran out the door.

"Why do you want to go to school with us?" asked Luna.

"For the shopping, of course!" their grandmother answered.

Claire almost choked on her Lucky Oats. She looked at Luna, who shrugged. While Grandy was basically a friendly witch, and a friendly grandmother, her Old School ways were sometimes unpredictable.

"She might be only going online shopping,

using the school computers," suggested Luna as they trooped out the door, Justin already two blocks ahead and Wilbur, chewing on a bottlecap, taking up the rear.

"Or she might be a serious encumbrance," said Claire. *Encumbrance* was her new favorite word. It made a wonderful bumbling sound that gave her a picture of an elephant balancing on a cucumber. "What do you think she's carrying that orchid for?"

Luna sighed. "I wish I knew."

Kids began to stare as soon as they passed through the fifth-grade doors. Usually parents, grandparents, and other grown-ups came though the front doors. (And cats were not allowed through any doors.)

"Let's stick together," Claire murmured to Luna. "Maybe we'll luck out and she'll want to go to Justin's room."

Unfortunately, Grandy and Wilbur headed right for 5A.

"Ah, yes," said Grandy, looking around with glee as she stepped into the room.

"Paradise. It reminds me of my honeymoon with my poor, lost Fred." She rubbed her hands together. "Plenty of bartering to be done here."

The room had changed in the weeks since Ms. Fleegerman had arrived. She had redecorated it to look just like Hawaii. There was a relief map of all the Hawaiian islands on the cork board, as well as papier-mâché flowers, colorful tissue leis, and magazine pictures of Hawaii tacked into every corner. Claire loved-loved-loved Ms. Fleegerman's dramatic touches, such as the basket of spiky protea flowers by the pencil sharpener and the big Styrofoam volcano on the windowsill. In fact, sometimes Claire wished that she, not Luna, had been the one allowed to stay in 5A.

But Ms. Fleegerman herself was a rules-and-regulations teacher, and she did not look pleased to have Grandy march into her classroom without so much as a permission slip.

"May I help you?" asked Ms. Fleegerman, standing up from her desk.

"I am Arianna Bramblewine," said Grandy. "Nice to meet you." She stuck out her hand.

Ms. Fleegerman took her hand to shake. Quickly, Grandy seized and squeezed it, hopped on one foot, and cast:

Freeze this minute to its death—

Everybody, hold your breath!

Time will stop so I might see

The riches of my shopping spree.

With harm to none,

This spell's begun.

This was a powerful five-star spell (imagine how hard it would be to freeze time!), and even a witch like Grandy could keep it going for only sixty seconds, maximum.

The next minute's silence was frightening. Claire and Luna (who were exempt from the spell) both shivered. All the kids were poised in place. Derrick Sherron was in the middle of picking his nose. Jemina Consolo was brushing her hair. Ms. Fleegerman was stopped mid-handshake, her eyes fixed on her notebook to see how she could have missed this appointment with Arianna Bramblewine.

Grandy shook off Ms. Fleegerman's grip. Then she whisked among the desks, cackling and muttering to herself.

"My tiger-frog orchid is so valuable, I can exchange it for anything without any hassle. The question is, what do I want in return? Hmm, these magazine pictures are nice. Or what about that nice volcano to brighten up my library? I must say, teachers have become quite talented at what they can do with your basic plain, four-cornered room."

Then Grandy spied Frieda Gunderson, frozen in the middle of copying the morning spelling words. Her mouth was dropped open in the start of a yawn, and her eyes stared sleepily at the blackboard.

Grandy's own eyes lit up. "Maybe I'll take that girl," she said to Claire with a little wink. "She looks like hard worker. And I need somebody to help me with my tomato plants."

"No, Grandy, please! Don't take Frieda!"

Claire pulled on Grandy's wrist.

"I bet I wouldn't even have to feed her much," Grandy mused. "Maybe a handful of oyster mushrooms now and then."

"Grandy," Luna said in her strictest voice. "Stealing Frieda is not a good idea."

"Oh, you girls are too serious for your own good!" Grandy snapped. "Child-snatching was outlawed from the Decree at least five hundred years ago. But I'm not going back from my shopping trip empty-handed, and my time-spell is running out. Eh, what're these?"

Over the blackboard, Ms. Fleegerman had taped up cutout letters from all different colors of construction paper. The letters spelled out:

IN HAWAII, ALOHA MEANS HELLO AND GOOD-BYE!

"Now, that's handiwork!" Grandy reached up and plucked off the first I. "She did this with nail scissors. Very dedicated. Okay, I'll take them." In a blink, she pulled off all the letters from the wall and stuffed them into her silver-buckled black purse. She had just buckled it shut and plunked her tiger-frog orchid smack in the middle of Ms. Fleegerman's desk when time unfroze.

Everybody continued what they were doing, from word copying to nose picking to hair brushing.

"Arianna Bramblewine? Are you the woman who is giving the assembly with the trick monkeys?" asked Ms. Fleegerman.

"What? Oh, for goodness' sakes, no. I'm a cat person." Grandy lifted her chin. "But since you asked, as a matter of fact, I'm the regional school inspector," she said mischievously.

"Really!" Ms. Fleegerman began to flip through her teacher's notebook. "Mrs. Hass did not say you were coming! I had no idea . . . I would have made some special preparations. I hope my classroom presentation is satisfactory." She looked around the room, then drew a sharp breath. "My letters are gone!"

"What letters?" asked Grandy, more mischievously.

"My aloha letters," said Ms. Fleegerman. She pointed to the empty space where the letters had been. "They were just there, a minute ago. Class! Class!" Her voice was shrill. "Would whomever took my letters kindly return them to me!"

The first bell rang.

"Oh, where does time go? I'm usually finished roll call by now." Ms. Fleegerman shook her wristwatch and held it to her ear. She glanced at her roll book. "Why, where did this orchid come from?"

"Compliments of the Inspectors' Bureau. Now, then, I must be getting on," said Grandy, "but as regional school inspector, I should warn you, madam, that you seem both disorganized and overly emotional. Come along, Wilbur."

With that, Grandy picked up Wilbur (who had fallen asleep in the trash basket) and swept out.

Ms. Fleegerman watched her leave, then wilted behind her desk. Out of the corner of her eye, she saw Claire and Luna. "Whichever one of you is Claire Bundkin, please go to your classroom," she said in her regular strict old Ms. Fleegerman voice.

"See ya," said Claire. She felt bad. It had been mean for Grandy to exchange those letters without telling. Claire knew that Ms. Fleegerman was having a hard enough time in 5A without having her words taken. Some kids called her Fleegermonster, and of course everyone wanted Mrs. Sanchez back. In fact, when Mrs. Sanchez had popped in last week for a quick visit and to show off her new baby, Olivia, 5A had gone berserk, jumping all around and hugging her.

Nobody would jump around and hug Fleegermonster. No way.

The truth was, it was perfectly possible for Ms. Fleegerman to think that any single one of the 5A kids had stolen her letters.

Later that morning, Ms. Fleegerman marched into 5B. "I will be putting this manila envelope on a chair outside my door," she said. "Would the person who borrowed my letters kindly put them in this envelope at his or her convenience?" she said. Her voice was haughty, but Claire knew that Ms. Fleegerman tended to get haughty when she felt unfairly treated. "My room is not the same without these letters," continued haughty-voiced old Ms. Fleegerman. "And I worked very hard to make it perfect."

A few kids snickered.

Claire did not snicker. She thought about the time she had practiced walking backward on her hands every afternoon for a month until she got it just right. Even though practice had roughened the skin off her palms and given her shoulder cramps, something inside her had needed to walk backward perfectly.

Claire bet that Ms. Fleegerman's feelings about her room were a lot like her own feelings about walking backward on her hands.

With the letters, 5A had been perfect.

A plan began to form in Claire's mind. On the way home from school, she told her plan to Luna.

"What? I don't want to waste my time

cutting out dumb letters. It would take forever," said Luna. "Besides, *Galaxy Murk* is on TV tonight."

"It's a repeat," said Claire.

"And since when is old Ms. F your best friend? She pushed you out of Five A! You should be happy that Grandy bought her letters!"

"Grandy *took* them," said Claire. "*Taking* is not the same as *buying*."

"She *exchanged* them," said Luna. "And exchanging *is* the same thing as buying. Almost."

"Is not."

"Is."

"Is not."

"Is, and either way," said Luna, "count me out. I don't like old Ms. Fleegerman, and I don't want to do her any freebie favors."

"You girls got some packages," said Grandy when they got home. Two identical brown-paper-covered boxes rested on the kitchen table.

The girls pounced and opened them. "Maybe this is something about the GSTs," whispered Claire.

But the packages turned out to hold their ugly bumblebee bridesmaids' dresses, newly fitted, from Regent's department store.

"Yick!" yelped Grandy. "What are these revolting bee costumes? It's not Halloween for another five months, three weeks, six days, and eight hours."

"Those are our junior bridesmaid dresses," said Claire.

"Did Furry pick them out?"

"Fluffy," corrected Luna. "And no, she didn't. We did."

"Well, what horrible picks," said Grandy. "You should be ashamed of yourselves. I'm going for a walk." She picked up her pigeon-shooer cane and whisked out the door.

The twins rushed upstairs to their room and tried on the dresses.

They were so ugly, they weren't even funny.

So ugly, that the only thing to do was to take them off. Fast.

"Maybe we *should* be ashamed of ourselves," Luna mentioned as she wriggled out of her dress. "Especially you. You picked them out."

"Who cares?" Claire swept the dresses into her arms and shoved them into the farthest back part of their closet. She slammed the closet door.

But she did care.

She decided to make up for it by doing something good.

"*I'm* cutting out letters," she said dramatically, her mind made up.

"Yuck. *I'm* not," said Luna, and she scooted out of the bedroom.

Claire sat on the floor and got out her ruler, colored construction paper, and her scissors. Thirty-three letters plus one comma, one hyphen, and one exclamation mark. Ugh! It would take forever.

With a long sigh, she began to trace the letters.

After about ten minutes, the bedroom door opened. Luna was holding their mother's first-aid kit scissors. She sat down next to Claire and gave a big long sigh of her own.

Claire handed her a few pieces of construction paper.

They worked until Grandy called them to dinner. They hurried through their homework and continued working until late into the night. They finished the last E and the ! a few minutes before they heard the cab pull up to the front door, and they were safe in bed just in time to get their good-night kiss.

The next morning, the girls ran to school very early. While Luna watched the hall, Claire poked the letters into the manila envelope.

Then they both dashed into 5A to see what would happen.

When Ms. Fleegerman walked into the classroom, she was holding the envelope. She shook the letters onto her desk. For a moment, her face melted with relief.

Then she looked closer. She seemed puzzled.

"Eggplants and eyeballs, she knows," Claire whispered. "Our letters probably weren't as good as the ones she made herself."

But if she did know, Ms. Fleegerman didn't let on. "I see the mystery borrower has returned my letters," she declared. "To that person, I would like to say thank you. Now, who will volunteer to help me tack them up?"

"I will," said Claire.

"I will," said Adam Chow, thinking that Claire was Luna.

"Good. Let's do it during lunchtime. And whichever one of you is Claire Bundkin, please report to Five B." Ms. Fleegerman's regular strict voice was back.

"See ya," said Claire.

Wasting lunchtime to do teacher-helping stuff was kind of unfair, Claire thought, but it didn't turn out to be all bad. Ms. Fleegerman brought a special lunch; some sandwiches, peanut butter cookies, and grape soda from the teacher's lounge.

When all the words were pinned back in the right place, Ms. Fleegerman surveyed the room.

"It's not Hawaii," she said, a bit dejectedly.

"All the kids say your room is the best decorated," Claire told her. "Honest."

"Really?" Ms. Fleegerman sounded surprised.

"Yep." Adam Chow nodded. "I think the person who took your letters didn't do it from meanness. He or she probably couldn't resist them."

"Exactly!" said Claire.

"I had never thought of it that way," said Ms. Fleegerman, who now seemed content to think of it exactly that way. Her face brightened, and she took a big bite of her cookie. "I love beautiful words like *aloha*," she confessed. Her voice was almost shy. "I always feel an early-morning Hawaiian breeze in that word."

"Another good word is *prickly*," said Claire before she could stop herself. "It would hurt your fingers to pick up that word."

"I like the word *besotted*," said Ms. Fleegerman. "It's a fat, sleepy word."

Claire had not exactly planned to have Ms. Fleegerman turn into her word friend. And kids sometimes gave Claire strange looks when Ms. Fleegerman called out "Heliotrope!" or "Pumpernickel!" or "Hugger-mugger!" whenever she saw Claire in hall rotation. (After becoming her word friend, Ms. Fleegerman never again mistook Claire for Luna.)

As well, Claire never again could see her as an awful word like *Fleegermonster*.

Which made the friendship, all in all, a change for the better.

Like the transformation of a haughty old caterpillar into a lovely *mariposa*.

7
The Princess and the Peep

THE FIRST WEEKEND of May was when Tower Hill Middle School's fifth and sixth grade would perform *The Princess and the Pea.* Since Luna and Claire both were involved with the play, they would have to miss their usual weekend in Bramblewine.

"Then you may come out next weekend," said Grandy.

"Are we especially invited?" asked Luna

worriedly. She wanted to make sure, after what had happened the last time.

"Yes," said Grandy. "You are extra-especially invited. And good luck with your play. Sorry I won't be there, but I hate-hate-hate school plays. There's always too much chorus singing."

Everyone else was coming. "Mom and Steve, Dad and Fluffy, and Justin." Claire ticked off the names on her fingers while she and Luna sat in the audience watching a dress rehearsal. Aside from being on crew—Claire for stage-managing and Luna for scenery painting—the twins had non-speaking roles as ladies-in-waiting in Act Three.

The rest of the time, they helped out by being the audience.

"We need to buy five tickets," said Claire. "Frogfeet and fiddleheads, I wish I could figure out a way to get Fluff seated behind someone really tall!"

"Mmm." Luna was not paying attention to Claire's schemes. She was listening to Angelica Antonio sing.

Angelica Antonio was a sixth grader. She had waist-length hair and wore ankle-length skirts, and she played the lead role of Princess Winifred, the princess who felt the pea under twenty mattresses.

"She's the greatest singer I've ever heard," said Luna. She wondered if Angelica Antonio would be available to sing at her wedding one day.

"She's also the snootiest girl in the sixth grade," Claire answered. "I can't stand how she swishes her hair over the back of her chair when she sits down. Hey, maybe we could put some chair-colored bubble gum on Fluffy's seat!"

Luna nodded distractedly. She was thinking of the perfect compliment to give Angelica after rehearsal. Something to express exactly how the music danced like butterflies in her stomach whenever she heard Angelica's voice.

But it was hard for Luna to speak up to people she didn't know. She decided to proceed with caution.

After rehearsal, she stood next to Angelica

backstage and tried to say her compliment. She stood there for a long time. She began to feel stupid. When Angelica turned to her and raised an eyebrow in a way that meant *why are you standing next to me?* Luna hurried off.

That night after dinner, Luna tried to sing as she dried the dishes. Just to test the sound of her own voice, which she did not remember as being very good.

"Uh, did you swallow a tongue depressor?" asked Justin. Then he and Claire laughed and gave each other high-fives.

"Shut up," Luna muttered. It didn't seem fair that a person who loved-loved-loved singing as much as herself should have such a bad, crackly voice.

The next afternoon at rehearsal, Luna had an idea. She was just finishing up some backdrop scenery for Act Two, which showed the palace hall. She had been painting a silver mirror. But in a burst of inspiration, she decided to turn it into a portrait of Princess Winifred.

She worked hard to get the portrait to

look like Angelica, with long hair and silvery musical notes floating from her mouth. As a final touch, she painted a tiger-striped kitten in Angelica's arms.

"Who's that supposed to be?" The sound of Angelica's voice made Luna turn with a start.

"Oh, I don't know," said Luna, stepping back and looking at the picture as if she just noticed it herself.

"It looks dumb to put a face there," said Angelica. "I liked it better when it was an empty window." Then she walked away before Luna could explain that it was not a window, but a mirror.

Quickly, Luna painted over the portrait and turned it into a window.

On the evening of the performance, Luna had another idea. She bought Angelica a white rose and a card. Inside the card she wrote, *I think you sing perfectly!*

She left the rose and note on the makeup table backstage, where Angelica would be sure to see it.

"Does anyone know gave this to me?" asked Angelica when she came into the dressing room. She held up the rose and spun around so that her hair swished. "Was it Zack? Adam? Peter? Who? Come on, guys! I know it was one of you!"

Luna could not bring herself to say anything. She kept her head down.

"See? That's what you get for being nice to snotty Angelica Antonio!" snapped Claire after Angelica left the dressing room. She turned so that Luna could button up the back of her lady-in-waiting costume. "Let me cast a throat-scratch spell on her!"

"Don't even dare." Now Luna turned so that Claire could button up the back of her costume. "That would wreck the play for everyone."

"Well, guess what I *did* do? I put a wobbly chair in the place where Fluffy's sitting. I peeked out into the audience and she looks all crooked! Ha ha!"

Luna was not really listening.

She waited until Act One was over before she steeled her nerve.

It was now or never.

Angelica was in the wings, sitting on one of the Styrofoam tree stumps and drinking hot lemon-and-honey water. Lindsey Berger, a sixth grader who played the Queen, was braiding Angelica's hair. (There was always one girl or another braiding Angelica's hair.)

"It's me who thinks you sing perfectly, Angelica," Luna said, so quiet she could hardly hear herself.

Angelica shrugged. "Okay," she said. Then she realized. "Oh, you were the one who gave me that card and the rose. Thanks, Claire."

"I'm Luna," said Luna.

Angelica smiled in a way that didn't really look like a smile at all. "Listen. Luna. That's nice of you and all, but sixth graders and fifth graders are like oil and water," she said. "They don't mix. Get it? No offense."

Lindsey Berger began to laugh, and then Angelica giggle-snorted. It was a mean, sixth grade giggle-snort, as awful as if Angelica had crushed the rose underneath her shoe.

Luna couldn't think of a thing to say. Her eyes felt hot. She hurried off.

She watched Act Two from the wings. Angelica's voice still was beautiful.

That almost made it worse.

In Act Three, when she and Claire were onstage for the Princess's royal wedding, Luna forgot all the chorus lyrics. She did not even remember to mouth along. All she could hear was Angelica's giggle-snort.

"Luna Bundkin, you sure got a case of cold feet out there," said Mr. Rosenthal in the lobby after the show. He clapped a hand on her shoulder. "Stage fright, hmm? I guess that's one way to tell you from your sister."

"I guess." Luna swallowed.

Her parents and Steve and Fluffy all looked at her sympathetically. It was embarrassing.

I will never do a single nice thing for anybody, ever again, Luna thought as she lay in bed that night. No More Nice. That would be her new policy.

The next morning, the sound of Angelica's giggle-snort had not left Luna's memory.

"Crumbs, Loon, you're still thinking about that? Who cares about snotty Angelica Antonio's giggle-snort?" Claire scoffed. "But if it really gets to you, cast a little itching-pink-eye spell on her. I won't tell Grandy." She grinned and rubbed her hands together. "In fact, I cast one on Jemina Consolo after she stole my rainbow eraser."

"Mmm." Luna pretended to agree, but it wasn't a witching revenge that she felt. It was a sadder feeling.

All week, whenever she saw Angelica, it was as if she was trapped in that same awful minute of the giggle-snort. It hurt the same amount.

No More Nice, thought Luna.

The next weekend, rain poured over the city. A tornado watch was on.

"May is coming in like a lion!" squealed Claire.

"No way I'm going to Bramblewine," said Justin. "It's even worse there when you're stuck indoors. Tell Grandy I have a debate competition."

"Maybe you girls should take a *rain* check on Bramblewine, too," joked their mother. (Most doctors tell pretty bad jokes.)

"We'll be fine!" Luna said. She was still upset about Angelica. At least at Bramblewine, she could cast a few grumpy spells in this witching weather. Grandy had promised to teach them how to shake branches down from the trees. Or, with Claire's help, she could send a mini-clap of thunder across the sky.

After layering them in raincoats and hats and preparing a thermos of hot cider, their mother dropped them at the station. The twins sat together in the train, passing the cider back and forth. The train creaked and swayed, and the lights flickered.

"I never took the train in a rainstorm," said Claire. "It's scary cool!"

To Luna, it was just scary. The trees bent in the wind. Rain hammered the top of the car. The conductor's shoes squeaked as he walked down the aisle.

"Maaay-rose!"

"Siiilver-toad!"

Men and women collected their umbrellas and blundered into the howling weather. The train chugged on.

"Laaang-ham!" the conductor shouted.

As always, the only person left was the man in the old-fashioned hat and the pea coat. As always, he was sleeping.

"Poor thing, he doesn't have an umbrella," murmured Claire. "I wonder why he didn't remember one? He might catch a cold. If I hadn't lost my umbrella, I'd sure lend him mine." She looked at her sister meaningfully.

Luna clutched her own umbrella. She did not want to lend it. It would go against her new policy of No More Nice.

Besides, it was never a good idea to talk to strangers.

Yet after so many years spent riding the train with the old man, he did not seem exactly like a stranger to Luna. He seemed more like a very nice old gentleman who would be soaked the minute he got off the train.

The train creaked around a narrow bend, and just as he always did, the man woke up with a start. Which, come to think of it, was pretty strange, Luna thought. How did he know to wake up at the same exact moment, every time?

She decided to put her No More Nice policy on hold for now. She stood up and walked down the aisle.

"Excuse me, would you like to borrow our umbrella?" she asked the old gentleman. "My sister and I already have hats and raincoats. Our mom is a doctor, and she's strict about cold and flu protection."

The man looked at her. He had eyes the color of warm chocolate chips.

"A doctor, hmm? She must be an intelligent

woman," he said. His hands closed around the offered umbrella. "If you're sure you don't mind, then I thank you kindly. Are you getting off at the next stop?"

"No, we're the last stop. Bramblewine."

"Ah, Bramblewine," said the old man sadly. "That's where I'd like to go. But for some reason I keep jumping off at Dillweed."

"Then what do you do?" asked Luna.

"Why, I catch the next train and loop around again," he said. "I've been doing this for a few hours. Let me tell you, it's quite frustrating. Well, it was a pleasure to meet you, young lady." He stood, reached for her hand and shook it.

Luna looked hard at the old gentleman. Something about him seemed familiar.

"Diiill-weed," hollered the conductor.

"Unfortunately, that's my stop," said the old man with a sigh.

"No, it's not, remember?" Luna clutched the old man's hand. He tried to shake free of Luna's grip.

"Is so," he said.

"Is not!" She held on. Her heart was pounding. Because she *knew*.

Claire, who had been watching from her seat, jumped up and rushed over. "Luna, you loon, let go," she ordered.

"Clairsie, look into his eyes. Don't you see who he is?"

Claire looked closer. She gasped. Then she said, "Who?"

"Our very own grandfather, Fred Bramblewine, that's who," whispered Luna in Claire's ear. "It's Grampy!"

"Please let go of my hand, miss," said Grampy. "The train is in the station!"

"I think he's stuck in some sort of repeat-mistake loop," said Luna. "We've got to spring him. Take his other hand, Clairsie, and do a number three-five-oh!" (Just like doctor's procedures, most witch spells have shorthand, in case of an emergency.)

Claire took his other hand. Rapidly, they chanted:

Time can fly when you're having fun

Or it can stutter and come undone

A sudden slap might do the trick

Fred Bramblewine, *from time, unstick!*

And then Luna slapped her long-lost grandfather across the face.

"Miss, that wasn't very nice!" he sputtered. "And I missed my stop!"

Sure enough, the train was creaking past Dillweed to its final destination.

"No no no, I haven't missed my stop," said Grampy, squinting out the window. "I'm supposed to get off . . ."

"With us," finished Luna.

"With you?" He looked startled.

"Trust us," said Claire.

It would be hard to explain the look on Grandy's face when the girls got off the train, each of them holding on to one of their grandfather's hands.

"Could that be . . . Is that my long-lost Fred, unstuck at last?" she asked. She came closer, then touched his face carefully, as if he might break. Then she gave a whoop and hugged him very hard. And in spite of Grampy doing his best to hold Luna's umbrella over them all, everyone got very wet from rain and tears.

As soon as they got to the house, Grandy phoned their mother, who immediately made plans to drive over with Justin.

"Serves me right. It's all my fault for trying to Change Destiny," Grandy told the girls privately, after Grampy had gone upstairs to take a much-needed bubble bath. "You see, Fred was always falling asleep on his commute, nightclub singing being a rather late-night job. I thought I was helping him out when I cast a spell that would always wake him up at the last stop. But I forgot one important thing—that *Dillweed* is generally thought to be the last stop, not *Bramblewine*. Bramblewine is the *secret* last stop."

"And to think we saw him for years and years, and never suspected a thing," said Luna.

"I know." Grandy shook her head ruefully.

"But think how hard it was for me to know dear Fred was riding the train around and around for nearly a decade. I was powerless, though. It's the standard punishment for Destiny Changing—once it's done, there's no undoing a miscast spell. But now he's home, thanks to you smart girls. I *knew* you'd unstick him one day!"

"Ten years," said Claire. "That's a long time to be away."

"Luckily for Fred, the ride only seemed like a few hours."

The girls looked confused. Grandy explained. "When you are inside a repeat-mistake-loop, you're also riding on top of a time current. It's the same as not being able to tell how deep the ocean gets when you're swimming in it. But I'll have to pop Fred full of some memory spells, just so he knows who won the World Series and how many grand-children he has." Grandy put her hand on her heart and sighed. "It would devastate Fred to know he'd been gone so long from the family. Meantime, hide any calendars if you see them."

They went out to the kitchen to cast a quick lunch before their mother and Justin arrived.

"Mom, you must have been cooking for hours!" exclaimed Jill Bundkin when she and Justin walked into the kitchen. "You should teach a time-management class at my hospital!"

"I just hope it tastes good!" Grandy smiled (because of course it all would taste delicious).

After lunch, everyone gathered in the living room. Grandy played piano and Grampy sang for them. He had a wonderful voice, too, Luna thought. Different from Angelica Antonio's, but it had the same amount of perfect. And Grampy made a far better choice to sing at her wedding.

She was glad she had broken her No More Nice rule.

"This is like old times," said their mother happily. "Oh, Dad, I'm just overjoyed that you decided to come home from wherever you were."

"What do you mean?" asked Grampy. "I was only in Philadelphia."

"Remind me to toss some memory spells into your mother and brother, too," Grandy whispered to the girls.

Outside, the wind howled as the storm raged.

"Wolf weather," said Justin. And he let out his usual howl that made the girls cover their ears.

"I can do that, too," said Grampy, and let out a howl of his own.

Justin did a louder howl.

Then Grampy and Justin howled together.

"I suppose we'll be seeing more of you out here in the future, young man," said Grandy, looking pleased, even as she covered her ears.

8
Edith and Hortense

CLAIRE KNEW it was going to happen anyway.

In spite of the boycotting.

In spite of the bumblebee dresses.

Their father and Fluffy were getting married on June fifth. Nothing was going to stop him.

"And of course, Fluffy *had* to get married over our Bramblewine weekend," said Luna.

"And of course, Fluffy *had* to pick First

Presbyterian, which we walk past on the way to school, so we have to be reminded about her dumb wedding every single day!" Claire rolled her eyes.

"And of course, Fluffy *has* to hold her reception at The Aubergine, so even Steve thinks she's a real princess." Luna sneered. "Fluffy should have got married in Texas after all, instead of *ruining* Philadelphia for the rest of us."

"Well, we're going to do some ruining ourselves," said Claire, rubbing her hands together.

Because something very nasty and ugly had dragged itself out of the brewing vats. The twins had decided that if they couldn't Destiny Change the fact that this wedding was going to happen, the next best thing was to make it the worst day possible.

With spells, of course.

"Good, Smart, Tricky spells," said Claire. "The kind of spells that will help us pass the GSTs and give us our stars and kittens." She was breathless at the meanness of it.

Late at night, they pored over their

Little Book of Shadows and made their plans. They cackled and snickered. They plotted and fumed. They worked and schemed very hard.

On the morning of June fifth, the twins were up with the sun to perform their first spell.

They stood outside on the front steps facing each other, each of them holding a daisy, and softly chanted:

Of flowered church
And flowered table
Fluff's done the best that she is able
All's decorated to the hilt.
Too bad the flowers have to wilt.

Then they used their thumbs to pop off the daisy heads.

This was a harder spell than it seems, because witches love-love-love gardens and flowers, and to wilt any plant deliberately goes against all witch-intuition.

(In fact, the spell made Claire feel a little sick.)

The next spell had to be performed in front of the refrigerator. While Luna held out her palm, Claire poured and stirred a teaspoon of sugar and a teaspoon of salt into it.

A tasty cake
With but one fault.
When sugar turns
Itself to salt.

"I didn't even know there *was* a wedding cake spell," said Claire.

"It's nothing compared to some of those spells in the 'Love's Revenge' chapter." Luna grimaced. "Brokenhearted witches can get pretty vicious."

The next and final spell needed to be performed at First Presbyterian Church, so it would have to wait until they all arrived. The girls quickly ate their Lucky Oats, then changed into their bumblebee bridesmaid dresses before they walked over with Steve and their mother (Justin, in his best man suit, ran a few blocks ahead).

"Frankly, I'm surprised Fluffy okayed those dreadful dresses," their mother commented as she studied her daughters. "Being that she's in the fashion industry and all."

"We told you. She loves them," said Luna.

Claire grinned behind her hand. That's when she noticed the fat pink wart that had sprung up on her palm.

"Ew! Look." She showed her sister.

Luna checked and saw she had a wart on her palm, as well.

"What do you think it means?" Claire asked. She inspected it carefully. "That we're getting closer to our stars?"

"I don't think so. Grandy doesn't have any warts," Luna answered. "To tell you the truth, I'm worried about our next and final spell. Isn't it awfully close to Destiny Changing?"

"Don't be such a worrywart. I'm sure we have a technical loophole," said Claire. She wasn't certain how, but she had heard the phrase on *Galaxy Murk* the other night and it seemed to apply nicely to this situation.

The church was empty. Quickly, the girls dashed up to the altar to cast their final spell, before they lost their nerve:

Forget you not.

Forget me, too.

Forget to say those words,

"I do."

"Well, methinks it's done," said Luna faintly.

"Hounds and hunchbacks, look, Loon!" Claire lifted her hands, palms up. Half a dozen little pink warts had sprouted. There was even one on her wrist.

"I've got 'em, too." Luna's lip curled. "Yuck."

"And look, the flower-wilt spell's in full force!"

They glanced around the church. It was true. Shabby roses were bent over the pews. Brown-edged hydrangeas and bunches of brittle baby's breath drooped in their altar vases.

Everything looked awful.

"This'll teach Fluff to steal other people's dads!" said Luna weakly.

They hurried back down the aisle and took their places in the church vestibule along with their father, who had asked them to help greet the guests.

"You look nice, Dad," said Claire.

"Thanks," he said. He fidgeted with his cuff link. "I hope everything goes smoothly. For some reason, the flowers are losing more steam every minute." He snapped his fingers. "Maybe it would help if the air conditioning were turned up. Yes, that's it!" He hurried away.

The church began to fill. Even Grandy and Grampy had come, Grampy in his velvet smoking jacket and Grandy with her silver dragon cane. A row of ladies all looking somewhat like Fluffy filed into one of the pews.

"Her four sisters, I guess," said Luna.

Then a very grand, proud couple walked in, smiling and waving.

"Fluff's parents, Mr. and Mrs. Demarkle," whispered Claire. They looked nice, she thought, remembering that Fluffy's parents already had invited the girls to come visit them.

Mr. Demarkle sat Mrs. Demarkle in the

pew, and then took his place by the door, waiting to escort Fluffy down the aisle. He tipped his hat to the girls.

"Shame that Edith Hortense's flower arrangements are doing so poorly," he said. "Let's cross our fingers that she won't notice."

But now other people were pointing to the dying flowers and whispering. Claire looked at Luna, who frowned and glanced away.

Claire knew what she was thinking. The flower-wilt spell was not quite as funny as they had hoped.

In fact, it wasn't very funny at all.

A sleek silver limousine pulled up in front of the church. In a bounce of white satin, Fluffy jumped out. She looked absolutely perfect. Her dress was swoopy, her hair was in ringlets, and her face shone with excitement.

Claire heard Luna gasp in delight. Her sister loved-loved-loved wedding dresses. Even Claire had to admit Fluffy looked pretty good.

The organist stuck up the opening chords of the wedding march.

Fluffy swept up the stairs and took Mr. Demarkle's arm. The smile on her face froze.

"What happened here?" she asked. "What happened to my flowers?"

"How about let's just get this wedding over with?" suggested Luna brightly.

"I'm not stepping a foot down this aisle until I know what happened to my wedding flowers!" Fluffy stamped her foot.

Heads turned around in the pews.

The music stopped.

Their father hurried from the altar up the aisle. His face was red.

"There seems to be a small problem with the flowers, Fluff," he said quietly. "It's the air-conditioning, I think."

"But this isn't at all how I pictured my special day." Fluffy's eyes were beginning to tear. She looked as wilted as the bouquets.

Claire felt terrible. She pressed a warty hand to her hot forehead. Maybe she could ask Grandy to cast a flower-fixer spell. (But that would be admitting a mistake, and that was no way to get a star!)

"I'll get the organ lady to play something lively while we take five," said Fluffy's dad. He strode off.

"We could grab a garbage bag and chuck 'em, Fluff, if you want," said Justin, who had come back to see what the commotion was all about.

"Yes," Luna agreed, stepping forward. "The church looks nice enough without flowers."

Fluffy raised a hand. "Please, gals. Don't come near me in those dresses," she implored. Her skin was already beginning to swell. "Oh, no!" she wailed, touching her hands to her face. "Excuse me. I think I better take a minute to cool off."

She picked up her skirt, stumbled outside, and plopped down on the church steps, her head in her hands.

"Justin, you and I are going to find some trash bags and get rid of these flowers," said their father briskly. To the girls, he pointed his finger and said, "You two stay with Fluff."

As soon as the girls were left alone, Luna turned worried eyes on Claire. "Oh, Clairsie, there's *nothing* funny about this."

Claire looked at Luna and Luna looked at Claire. Neither of them liked what they saw; a frowning girl in a bumblebee dress up to her wrists in fat pink warts.

"I was thinking," Luna began softly. "You know how sometimes you try to do the right thing, but instead it gets scrambled up by accident into something wrong? Like Justin's love powder. That was an honest mistake."

"Or, sometimes doing the right thing doesn't get you any credit. Like making old Ms. Fleegerman her new letters," Claire reflected. "But we did it anyhow. And then there's doing something right that make you feel worse, like your rose for Angelica."

"But sometimes, the right thing gives back a thousand times, like with Grampy," Luna said. "We lent an umbrella, and we got back a grandfather!"

"And sometimes," Claire said slowly, "sometimes doing something right is more like making a good investment in the future. I mean, if Fluffy steals Dad to Texas, we can't do anything to stop her."

"Right," agreed Luna reluctantly.

"Because no matter if we're in Philadelphia or Houston, Fluffy's part of our family now. It's her Destiny, whether we like it or not."

"Right," agreed Luna.

They were silent for a moment. It was the closest the twins had ever come to a moment of ESP. Then they knew exactly what to do.

They linked pinkies and walked outside.

Fluffy was still slumped on the steps, her head in her hands.

"Hey, Fluff." As Claire spoke up, she placed her hand dramatically on her heart. "Please don't be sad. We can fix this."

Fluffy turned. Her face was teary and puffy. "Gals, step back. I mean it. My complexion can't handle those darn bee dresses."

"Give us fifteen minutes, okay, Fluffy?"

asked Luna. "We promise we can undo everything."

Fluffy dropped her head back into her hands. "We should have eloped to Las Vegas," she muttered.

It was no use talking to her. The twins dashed back into the church and pulled their mother from the pew.

"Mom, maybe you could ask Grampy to sing a few songs from his nightclub act to distract the congregation? There's going to be a small delay," Luna explained.

"Oh, dear," said their mother. "Fluffy's got last-minute cold feet?"

"Something like that," said Claire.

They ran out of the church and down the block. Tower Hill Middle School was always open on the weekends, for sports and band practice. They dashed backstage and tore off their bumblebee costumes. Then they put on their *Princess and the Pea* ladies-in-waiting costumes. Luna buttoned up Claire and Claire buttoned up Luna.

"Much better," Luna said.

On the way out the door, they passed by 5A to pick up the decorations. They did not expect Ms. Fleegerman to be at her desk.

"What are you girls doing here?" she asked.

"We're going to a wedding and we had to change into our bridesmaid dresses. What are you doing here?"

"I'm correcting papers," said Ms. Fleegerman.

She tried to look strict, but only managed to look lonely.

"Actually, we were looking for you, Ms. Fleegerman. We wondered if we could borrow some of these classroom decorations," said Claire. "Our dad is getting married in ten minutes."

"Well, I never planned on lending these out," said Ms. Fleegerman.

"It's sort of an emergency," explained Luna. "All the wedding flowers died. Something to do with the air-conditioning."

"Oh, that's a shame." Ms. Fleegerman looked around her room. "I always did think it was too bad that nobody except fifth graders could see these decorations." Her brow furrowed. "I'm not really dressed for a wedding, but . . . all right. I'll bring them over."

"Thanks, Ms. Fleegerman!" they chorused. Quickly, they bundled up the basket of proteas and other decorations into boxes. Then, with minutes to spare, they dashed back to the church.

Inside, it did not look very wedding-ish. Accompanied by the organ, Grampy was singing "Old Black Magic" while Justin walked up and down the aisle tossing the dying flowers into a big green trash bag. People were whispering and looking confused.

"Sugar, is there still going to be a wedding?" asked one of Fluffy's sisters.

"Absolutely," said Claire.

Carefully, the girls and Ms. Fleegerman strung the leis like garlands along the pews.

The congregation *oooh*ed when Ms. Fleegerman placed her potted proteas on the altar. Fluffy, who had crept back inside the church, watched in wonder.

"Much better," said Claire, surveying the church. She gave her dad a thumbs-up and nodded to the organ player.

Everyone took their places.

The wedding march started.

The girls walked tall.

And Fluffy looked radiant.

It wasn't until Fluffy and their father were standing at the altar and the minister asked for the rings that the girls remembered.

The vow-forget spell!

"I don't know how to undo it," Claire whispered through gritted teeth.

"Try thinking of love or something," Luna whispered back.

Claire thought of all the things she loved-loved-loved. Gymnastics and Hawaii and the word *hugger-mugger*.

Luna thought of all the things she loved-

loved-loved. Painting and beautiful voices and Adam Chow, maybe.

They held their breath as the minister asked Edith Hortense Demarkle if she took Louis Bundkin to be her husband.

There was silence. A small silence that swelled to deafening pitch.

I do—I do—I do! thought Luna

I do—I do—I do! thought Claire.

"I do!" said Fluffy finally, in a happy jolt of remembering.

"I do!" said their father, even though it wasn't his turn, yet.

And that's when the girls learned something very important; that the power of love is far greater than the power of spells.

The groom kissed the bride, and everyone broke into cheers.

At The Aubergine, there was music and dancing. Their mother danced with Steve and Justin. Justin danced with the girls and Grandy. Grandy danced with Grampy, who also danced with their mother, Claire and

Luna, all of Fluffy's sisters, and even Ms. Fleegerman. And Ms. Fleegerman taught everyone how to do the hula.

"Gals, I don't know how you did it, but thanks for helping to make this the best day of my life!" Fluffy squeezed each twin tight.

"Anytime, Fluff," said Luna.

"Yep, you just tell us where and when, and we'll show up," added Claire with a grin.

Steve had whipped up a delicious banquet.

"This is the best veggie dip I ever had," said Claire. "I love it!"

"That's my special guacamole," Steve said. "The trick is to use fresh avocados."

Avocados! Quickly, Claire gulped a large sip of water.

"This was a very nice wedding dinner," complimented Grandy as she passed by the table where the twins were sitting. "I'm especially looking forward to the cake."

"It might not taste very good," said Claire sorrowfully, glancing across the room to where the spell-salted cake sat on its own table strewn with rose petals. "We hope everyone is in too good a mood to care."

Grandy smirked. She crooked her pinkie toward the cake and chanted:

Your warts tell stories of defeat

That twinnies have been less than sweet.

A salty cake will taste all wrong

Come back, sweet cake, and warts, so long!

"How did you know?" asked Claire, watching with relief as her warts shrank up and disappeared.

"A grandmother knows these things," Grandy said. "But I am proud of you girls. Today, you did something good, smart, and tricky. Plus, you did it with wits, not witchcraft. Most importantly, you used love to undo a Destiny Change spell. And so . . ." Now Grandy was holding a wicker basket that seemed to have materialized out of nowhere. The twins hardly dared to look inside.

Curled up in the basket were the two most adorable striped kittens the girls had ever seen.

One was gray with black markings and one was black with gray markings. Around each of their necks was the prized silver star.

"And I have just the right names for them. Something to honor this special day." Luna leaned close and whispered in her sister's ear.

At first, Claire frowned. She loved the sound of beautiful words, and those names were not even pretty.

Then she thought about it a moment longer. Right now, sure, these kittens were adorable, but they would grow up to be working cats. Witch cats like Wilbur, who also had a plain (but serviceable) name.

No, adorable names would not suit these witch cats at all.

"Edith and Hortense," she said, staring into the basket. "I guess I could get used to those names. And these kittens *are* very fluffy."

Hortense stared up knowingly. Her humanspeak was already quite good.

And Edith closed one eye and yawned.